BLONDIE REQUITED

BLONDIE REQUITED

Tony Granger

Mentor

MFS Books

Cover Photograph of Anthony Granger with his grandfather Daniel Luckhoff -1954

Copyright © Tony Granger 2020

All rights reserved. No part of this publication may be reproduced, stored in a retrieval system, or transmitted in any form or by any means, electronic, mechanical, photocopying, recording, or otherwise without the prior permission of the publishers.

First published in 2020 by Tony Granger

11 Melbourne Rise, Bicton Heath, Shrewsbury, Shropshire SY3 5DA

Tel: 00 44 1743 360827 Email: tony@tonygranger.com

Printed and bound in Great Britain by 4edge Ltd of Hockley, Essex, England

www.4edge.co.uk

Published by Mentor Financial Services Limited as MFS Books

This book is sold subject to the condition that it shall not, by way of trade or otherwise, be lent, resold, hired out, or otherwise circulated without the publisher's prior consent in any form or binding or cover other than that in which it is published and without a similar condition including this condition being imposed upon the subsequent purchaser.

British Library Cataloguing in Publication Data is available

ISBN 978-1-9163125-1-7

About the Author

Tony Granger lives in Shrewsbury, Shropshire, England. He was born in South Africa in 1951, and moved to Rhodesia in 1958 with his family, where he grew up, attending schools in Salisbury and Sinoia before moving back to South Africa to read economics and law at Rhodes University in Grahamstown.

During his first degree, Tony developed an entrepreneurial flair and bought a farm in Grahamstown, Eastern Cape, South Africa farming anything that began with a 'P' – pigs, pineapples, proteas, prickly pears – and had a couple of cows for milk. The main farmhouse was let out to students and he converted the dairy into a cottage where he lived. In addition to this he worked as assistant manager at the Settlers Inn Motel for extra pocket money whilst a student.

In 1973 he returned to Rhodesia to join the British South Africa Police (BSAP), feeling that a police career could augment his advocacy skills later. Serving first as a District Policeman in uniform branch, he later transferred to the CID and then to Special Branch, where he was mostly engaged in anti-terrorist operations during the 1970s as guerrillas stepped up their infiltration of Rhodesia.

Returning to South Africa, Tony completed an LLB degree and was admitted to the Bar in Cape Town as an Advocate of the Supreme Court. Shortly thereafter he joined the Old Mutual Group as a legal adviser rising through the ranks into divisional management. He was awarded the Chairman's Prize in 1986.

Moving to England in 1987, he became an independent financial adviser and headed up a number of companies in the financial services world. Seeing a wide gap in the training of accountants, solicitors and IFAs in financial planning he formed the first financial services training company in the UK and began writing financial books on pensions, inheritance tax, investments, corporate planning, school and university fees and other publications. Of his 18 books to date, the latest one was a Bereavement Guide, and this is to be followed by a Later Life Planning Guide due for publication 2021.

Tony is a Trustee of the Rhodes University (UK) trust and was awarded the Distinguished Old Rhodian Award in 2017;

Almoner of the BSAP Regimental Association (UK) and Trustee of the BSAP Trust; Trustee of the Zimbabwe Pensioners Support Fund (UK); Member of the International Police Association (IPA). He is a Fellow of the Royal Society of the Arts, Manufactures and Commerce, and a Freeman of the City of London through the Worshipful Company of International Bankers. A past President of the Financial Planning Institute of Southern Africa (FPI), and the CII in Shropshire and Mid Wales, he maintains a strong interest in the development of new financial products and ideas to make lives better for people. He is a member of and works with the Chartered Institute of Securities and Investment (CISI) in setting and moderating exam papers in financial planning and is a visiting Professor at London Metropolitan University. Involved in environmental issues and the reduction of harmful greenhouse gases, Tony is the author of a leading report on carbon credits and greenhouse gas emissions and believes that there are cheaper more cost-effective methods for immediate reduction of air pollution.

Tony has also written a number of Murder Mystery Plays and children's stories.

Tony was married to Joy who died of cancer in 2008 and has two sons – James, a teacher and Chris, a doctor. He is blessed with three grandchildren.

This book is dedicated to my family and many friends from school, university, playing rugby and police force days.

Preface

Blondie Requited is a book of short stories that follows on from a similar book in the same vein – Blondie's Revenge, first published in 2006 with over thirty reprints and still very much in demand today. I fully believe that humour enlightens our lives and many of the stories in this book have an element of humour running through them. Most concern past events in my life from school and university days through to my days as a policeman in Rhodesia and my first murder investigations, and the extremely strong sense of justice imbued in ordinary people. Imagine an elderly father walking over sixty miles to report the murder of his grandson by the hand of his daughter; or the exhumation of a poisoned victim with a hostile crowd surrounding you trying to stop you at all costs.

Many will remember the adventures they had whilst hitch-hiking or whilst growing up and experiencing their first sex education lesson, or the trials and tribulations of their first driving experience, and happy holiday times. Others will be involved in genealogy and finding out about their fathers and grandfathers and what they did in their lives. I include a short war history of my own father in the second world war, and one of his published war poems. My grandfather on my mother's side of the family was a chaplain to the Boer women and children in one of the first British concentration camps during the Boer War, and the daily ordeals suffered by them and recorded by him in his diary make for heartfelt reading.

In my work life and playing sport I seemed to attract people with delightful senses of humour, and I have included some anecdotal stories from those times. Playing rugby has brought me into contact with many different characters from around the world, and the stories that are yet to be told will be a book on their own!

I am often asked why I write short stories and not full- length novels. Having written mainly financial books in the past, one develops a process of writing technically where the mind-set is completely different from lovely flowery prose – short stories flow easier for me and as a book genre are in short supply generally – yet people like them as each story is not too time consuming.

In Appreciation

I am indebted to the following for their help in making this book possible.

My proof- readers who were a great help, including **'Baby Binks'**.

Fran Stiff for her helpful advice.

Madelain Davies for her artwork and formatting.

4Edge my printers in the United Kingdom – you are always so efficient and helpful and really do make a difference.

Friends Trish Brownlow Chisnall, Angy Pare', Charlotte Swart and Fred Hammond for their useful comments and encouragement. Veronica Murdoch-Eaton for her encouragement to get the book out – she handles book sales for a number of authors.

My sons **James** (with Anna, Theo, Zara and Max) and **Chris** (and Louise) – 'hey dad when is the next one coming out – we need more Oupa stories for the children!'

To my good friend Gwyn Lewis who is a constant source of encouragement in most things.

Contents

		Page
1.	Driving from an Early Age	14
2.	Palmiet – Early Days	26
3.	Helga Giving Me Sex Education	38
4.	Taking a Body to Soweto	46
5.	Hitching a Ride	57
6.	BSAP Patrols – my first station	70
7.	The Last Foot Patrol	84
8.	Marrying a Known Terrorist	101
9.	Children's Pets	110
10.	Pofadder	113
11.	Helping Nelson Mandela select his Jumble	124
12.	There's a Bomb Under My Pedals	130
13.	50 Years of Rugby	136
14.	Are Writers Philosophers?	149
15.	Unmarked Grave	152
16.	War Poetry – Denis Granger in the Western Desert	164
	Glossary	173
	Epilogue	174

1

Driving from an Early Age

As little kids didn't we just love getting behind the wheel of the car, make vroom vroom noises and practice our driving? Not that we could see over the dashboard, nor could our feet touch the pedals, but we knew where the horn or hooter was as well as the indicators. My big driving ambition at the age of three and a half was to be as mobile as possible. Having moved from the stage of sitting on a potty and scooting it all around the house – we had parquet floors in those days, guaranteeing a smooth ride – I graduated to the tricycle, a fine Triang model.

At that time, the family lived at number 8 Theron Avenue, in Worcester on the edge of the Karoo in South Africa. The Karoo itself is semi-desert. We lived on a hill and behind the house was open veldt, with flowering Namaqualand Daisies in the spring, as well as gazanias, ursinias and vygies (mesembs) - fig-like plants resembling stones. All burst into colourful flowers in the spring and summer. In winter, (June to August) is the time of the year when most aloes are in flower.

Looking north from the house, the backdrop is the 2,000 m Brandwacht Mountain, often covered in snow. This mountain forms part of the Hex River Mountain system. Crystal clear water came running down from the mountains and through the town, and on many a hot day we would walk bare foot in these canal gullies beside the roads. Worcester itself lies in the Bree River valley between the Hex River and Du Toits Kloof mountains.

I had lost my older sister Melanie-Anne to a hole in the heart at a very young age, and when I was three my sister Debbie was born in 1954 and later Angela in 1958. My Dad, Denis Rhodes Granger was a Rhodesian born in Gwelo (now Gweru) in 1911 who practised law in Worcester and throughout the Karoo in places like Beaufort West, Colesburg and Calvinia. Dad was named after Cecil Rhodes, founder of Rhodesia and Prime Minister of the Cape. Dad was much interested in theatre and produced plays in Worcester, which is how he met my mother,

Isabeau Marguerite Luckhoff, who auditioned for one of his plays, when she was a reporter on the Worcester Standard newspaper. Mother was born in Stellenbosch in 1925, where her father dominee (Reverend) Daniel August Luckhoff was a church minister. Her mother was Sarah (Sally) Elizabeth (Joubert) Luckhoff.

My own roots were very deep Rhodesian and South African, and the spirit of adventure was ingrained in me.

So much so that I set off on the aforementioned tricycle to town, heading for the cinema known as the Good Hope Café and Scala Bioscope, at the tender age of 3½. I had no idea what else was there but knew that plenty of sweets were to be found. My mother was totally unaware that I had taken off at high speed and was shocked to get the call from the manageress of the Scala saying that I had arrived! I know that Dr. Spock's Baby & Child Care did not deal with cases of such magnitude and I was probably deprived of a jam sandwich or two for my escapades. I gave it a few years, and then decided that car driving was far more exciting. So at around the age of 6…

Driving from an Early Age

It was a Sunday afternoon and the Granger household was in lockdown. After Sunday lunch the children were banished to their bedrooms and the Parents retreated to theirs. They locked their bedroom door. After an hour or so, my sister and I crept up to their bedroom and tried to get in. Nothing doing. In fact,' silence'. That meant the folks were up to something. But what? Immediate thoughts of some unwrapped present or little treasure meant for us came to mind. This made us more determined. My sister had a good line in whimpering designed to bring immediate attention, and she and I began banging on the door saying 'let me in, let me in' – still nothing doing. This heightened our suspicions even more. They wanted to hide something from us – but what?

Eventually my father, obviously totally unnerved at this attempt at coitus interruptus, began threatening all sorts of punishment if we did not desist and go back to bed to rest. This made us even more determined as my sister then raised her level of whimpering and me the level of door banging. So much so that he said from the other side of the door we would get a lovely reward if we went back to rest. So we did. But not for long.

Blondie Requited

I decided it was time to do some driving and headed out of the house to where the family Ford Prefect sat outside number 8 Theron Avenue, on the roadside, facing up the hill. Nobody locked anything in those days, so entry was easy. I moved the seat forward and obtained a firm grip on the steering wheel. Vroom! Vroom! I shouted and did some solid steering. Wow this was fun! I had seen Dad disengage the handbrake so thought I knew what to do – and did it. The next thing the car was rolling slowly backwards, with me steering like mad – I couldn't see where I was going but somehow the inside wheels were following the curb as the car went downhill backwards, moving faster and faster!

At the bottom of the hill the road was a T junction where one could go left or right but not straight. However, straight is where I went – mounted the curb on the other side of the road, through a hedge and into the swimming pool of the house at the junction. Good friends of the folks', no doubt were also having siesta behind a locked bedroom door in their house. The back of the car was in the shallow end of the pool with the front wheels sticking up in the air. Boy did I get a fright! I was not prepared for this. I managed to clamber out through the car window and scrambled through a gaping hole in the hedge and back up the road as fast as I could, in through our front door and into my bed to feign sleep.

Half an hour later my father was up and about and asked who wanted to go for a drive to the Botanical gardens where there was a rescued Bambi on show. Sure we would love to go! They sold ice creams there and ever hopeful we would go anywhere for one. As we neared the end of our path to the road, my father noticed the car was no longer there. My mother, always the practical one, suggested it had been stolen – where else could it be? And to call the Police immediately. Konstabel du Toit duly arrived and took particulars of the vehicle. By now the neighbours at the bottom of the road had woken up and noticed a car, which they recognised as the Granger family saloon, having a swim in their pool. A quick call to the folks and down we all trooped down to view proceedings – a tow truck had been called. Konstabel du Toit said Hooligans must have done it. My father swore the hand brake was fully engaged when he left it. No one sought my opinion, so I remained blissfully quiet during this time of turmoil.

Thereafter my father put a brick behind the back tyre every time he parked, just in case.

Over the years people have asked me whether I confessed to TOC (taking of car), but I never did – until just before I got married and we were sitting around the camp fire telling stories, and I confessed. Whilst my mother reached for the Dr. Spock book of later confessed crimes, my father and I had a good laugh – he said he puzzled for years as to how his car had ended up in a swimming pool on a lazy Sunday afternoon.

Years later I was at it again. We had now moved to Rhodesia and I was about 12 years old. I lived in Marlborough, Salisbury, and had begun to take the beginning of a lifelong interest in girls. Everyone's house had a swimming pool, but the place to be was the Mabelreign swimming baths - about a 3 mile trip from where we lived, where we knew lots of girls would be partaking of the waters. So, we determined to go. We being Ian Mckenzie my next door neighbour, and his brother David. Ian's mother owned a mini car and was at work, the car being at home. Somehow the Mini was hotwired I think

Driving from an Early Age

by David (but with lots of advice from us) and we were set to go. I, being the tallest, was designated driver. So, along Salisbury Drive we went, up Marlborough Drive to the Lomagundi Road intersection which had to be crossed to get to Mabelreign. Next thing we were driving into a funnel of cones and brought to a stop by a very smart constable of the BSAP.

Roadblock! Oh no! 'Please may I see your licence sir?' asked the constable, ever so politely. 'Oh I must have left it at home' I responded. 'Is this your car?' 'No it belongs to my mother' I said. In no time at all we were found out, arrested and bundled into the police car and taken to the police station. Charges – taking of motor vehicle without permission, driving without a licence, driving under - age etc. Result - flogging of the Mckenzie boys by their father which sounded most severe from my place next door, and a severe dressing down from my parents who were as they say 'not amused'. I also had the charges to respond to in due course and wasn't even at high school yet! My father was a crack lawyer though and did his best. I remember giving Ian Mckenzie a bar of Brooklax chocolate (a very potent laxative which looks and tastes like chocolate) to make him feel better, as a thorough cleansing was called for.

I guess cars have always been a part of my life, and I have spent a fortune on buying them and having them repaired. After I married Joy we lived in Bindura, a small town about 40 miles north of Salisbury (now Harare). I owned a blue Triumph Spitfire car and a red MGA Sports car. The road from Salisbury (now Harare) and Bindura passed through farming area most of the way and had a few hot spots where cars had been ambushed, and one had to be very alert driving there. I was in the CID/SB in the British South Africa Police force at that time. Our womenfolk were trained in using the Israeli Uzi and also in handguns and when travelling always took a weapon with them. Joy was in the Triumph heading to Salisbury one day when it spluttered to a stop – right in the middle of ambush alley – and wouldn't start again when she tried to get it going. Luckily, Jerry Rickson, an SB friend, was driving towards Bindura at the time and came across the car and gave it a tow back to Bindura. On examination stones and pebbles were found in the petrol tank which had caused the vehicle breakdown. It later transpired that when I was in the CID drug squad, I had arrested someone for drug dealing, and this person, now out of jail, had seen me and the car in Bindura and had planted the stones in the petrol tank. I felt rough justice was called for, however never got the opportunity to dispense it!

I cannot let a car story go by without relating what I consider to be a miracle. After Joy and I decided to leave Rhodesia and head to South Africa (where I had been accepted at Rhodes University for a post graduate degree), I bought a Renault R12 from Neil Russell-Smith and a trailer which I had seen advertised. Into the trailer we loaded our worldly goods and headed for Fort Victoria (now Masvingo) to join the convoy to Beit Bridge. You had to arrive at a certain time, otherwise you would miss the convoy which had armed response protection against terrorist attacks. At that time, it was advisable not to travel on your own for fear of ambush. Note that once travelling the urge for going to the toilet intensifies. So it was for my wife. We had left Salisbury and reached Beatrice (about 35 miles away) when suddenly the car started to sway and the trailer began drifting across the road. I immediately stopped the car at the side of the road and saw that one of the trailer wheels was buckled. Joy leaped out and ran in to the bush at the side of the road for wee time and the next thing bullets and tracer rounds were flying all around us – we had driven into a contact area between the security forces and a group of terrorists. I do not know where I found the strength, but somehow managed to lift the trailer up, align it with the tow hitch and then slipped it off the hitch. We then leaped back into the car and drove into Beatrice, leaving the trailer behind, still fully loaded, on the roadside.

A mechanic later recovered the trailer back to Beatrice. The problem was that a wheel bearing had seized causing the wheel to buckle. The trailer axle was believed to be from a 1954 Consul car and there wasn't a hope in hell of finding a wheel bearing from that vintage in Beatrice or anywhere. As the tow hitch had also been damaged, I had to unpack the boot of the car to get at some tools. Amongst the tools I saw a wrapped-up oil cloth, and thought 'what is this?' Opening it up, there lay two - wheel bearings covered in grease. I asked the mechanic if these would fit the trailer wheel and he said he'd give it a go. It fitted perfectly. He hammered the tyre rim as straight as he could, and we were on our way. To this day I have no idea where those wheel bearings came from and why they should be in the tool section of a 1975 Renault. To me it was truly a miracle.

2

Palmiet – Early Days

As a boy I grew up in Worcester, Cape Province, South Africa. My mother Isabeau Granger was born to Sally and August Daniel Luckhoff in Stellenbosch in 1925. My grandfather, of German extraction, was born on 6 July 1874 in Colesburg in the Cape Colony and became a dominee (church minister) in the Dutch Reformed Church. He had been a missionary for most of his life, mostly amongst the Namaqua people in the northern Cape Province. He was chaplain to the Boer prisoners being held in British concentration camps during the Boer war (1899-1902). He wrote a book based on his diary, about his experiences in the Bethulie and other camps named 'Woman's Endurance'.

The Boer War was fought between the Boer (Afrikaner) Republics under Paul Kruger and the British Empire, represented by Field Marshall Lord Kitchener, an Irishman, who established the first concentration camps. Of the

Palmiet – Early Days

115,000 people in the camps, around 48,000 died, 22,000 of them children. This represented around 10% of the Boer population at the time.

My grandmother was Sally (Sarah Elizabeth – but called Sally) Joubert of French Huguenot and Dutch extraction. Her forebears had fled religious persecution in France, settling in South Africa. Due to the language laws in the Cape Colony at that time when my grandparents were courting, the only written word legally had to be in English, and I have copies of their courting correspondence – all in English! This surprised me as the lingua franca of the non-English speaking Europeans was either Dutch or Afrikaans. My grandparents had 5 children, Elise (Strydom), Anton Luckhoff (whom I am named after, who was also my godfather), Sadie (de Wet), Paul Luckhoff and my mother Isabeau (Granger), the youngest. In time, this became quite a big family. Elise had three sons, Boet, Danie and Gerhard and a daughter Elsa; Anton had two sons August and Abraham, who both became church ministers, and a daughter Cecelia; Sadie had four children – Sally, Paul, Elizabeth and Dan; Paul had two sons- Daniel who became a church minister and Paul a well-known actor. Isabeau had me Anthony, Deborah and Angela.

On my father's side, Dad was Denis Rhodes Granger, born in Rhodesia in 1911, when the country was less than 20 years old. He was named after Cecil Rhodes, Prime Minister of the Cape, and a contemporary of his father Joseph (Joe) Granger, who was persuaded to go to Rhodesia with the second wave of pioneers, by Rhodes. Joe Granger was born in Houghton-Le-Spring, near Durham in England, and came out to South Africa at the time of the gold rush to seek fame and fortune, along with his four brothers and later his sisters. He served in the Imperial Light Horse during the Boer War under Kitchener. My grandfathers had the distinction of being on opposite sides during the Boer War. During the First World War my grandfather Joe was gassed at Ypres and because of the poor condition of his lungs, was told to live at sea level. He then moved from Rhodesia to the Cape and later bought a house at St James in Cape Town, quite close to that of Cecil Rhodes.

I guess my heritage was typically South African. On the one side Afrikaners and on the other English. My father was

Palmiet – Early Days

practising as an attorney in Worcester, Cape, when he met my mother, then a reporter on the Worcester Standard newspaper. She had auditioned for a play he was producing, and the rest, as they say, is history. However, there was, I guess, some antipathy between my mother's parents and my father, especially so soon after the war. My mother's father because of his German lineage and with memories of the British concentration camps in the Boer War, did not have a particularly friendly disposition to the English. He was one of the Afrikaner trek leaders during the symbolic centenary Ox- Wagon Trek from Cape Town to Pretoria which began on 8 August 1938 in celebration of Afrikanerdom. This commemorated the Voortrekker (Afrikaner pathfinders) victory at the Battle of Blood River between 464 Voortrekkers under Andries Pretorius and some 15,000 Zulu warriors on the bank of the Ncome River (KZN) on the 16 December 1838. There were some 3,000 Zulu casualties and no Voortrekker losses.

I don't remember my mother's father ever speaking English to me, and I am sure he carried many bitter memories from past injustices. Anyway, I digressed to give a bit of family history before coming on to Palmiet.

Blondie Requited

The place Palmiet lies in the Kogelberg Nature Reserve alongside the Palmiet river in the area between Betty's Bay and Kleinmond in the Western Cape. It lies some 65 miles from Worcester (where I was born) and is about the same distance from Cape Town. On the edge of the nature reserve is the sea and a long beach, to the east of which is the Palmiet River and lagoon. Behind that are the Kogelberg mountains. The whole area is rich in proteas and other flora. The word Palmiet derives from a robust semi-aquatic plant that flourishes along the river banks. Prionium serratum is derived from the Greek prion meaning a saw and refers to the leaf blades, serratum to the toothed edges. The flower shoots can be eaten as a vegetable and the leaves used for basketry work.

Oupa (Grandfather) Luckhoff was given an 'outspan' piece of land by the South African Government at the edge of the beach overlooking the sea, as a reward for his missionary work in Namaqualand. This was in the Kogelberg Nature Reserve and being a nature reserve, building was prohibited other than at this outspan site.

The house he built was made using the timbers from a shipwreck washed up on the beach - the Gustav Adolf ship

Palmiet – Early Days

in July 1902. The Cape Times reported that the Norwegian barque was making for Cape Town from Fremantle, Australia with a cargo of sleepers and tar. Of the 11- man crew, the captain and three men drowned. The shipwreck occurred at the mouth of the Palmiet River. The ship had sprung a leak in stormy weather, with water 18 feet deep in the hold. The captain decided to run the ship ashore, onto the beach near the river mouth. However, it was wrecked on a reef and one of the lifeboats, of the two subsequently launched, was smashed to bits by a wave. The ship had one passenger (the others being crew) who drowned – a young man aged around twenty - William Perkins who was intending to make a new life for himself in Cape Town. The seven survivors were housed at Kleinmond by Mr. Albertyn.

The Palmiet house had a number of bedrooms, a kitchen, a storeroom, dining room and a stoep (verandah) which was partly enclosed and faced the sea. It was built mainly of wood and corrugated iron for the sides and the roof, which was pitched and had an upstairs storeroom accessed by an outside ladder. The roof was painted red and it became known as Die Rooidak huis (House with the red roof). It also had servants' quarters attaching to it. As the family grew, in years to come, Oupa built a smaller cottage next door to it for my mother and her family – this was known as the 'Kalfie'- a name given to a small calf – it was small indeed – 2 bedrooms and a front kitchen and dining area only. There was an outside toilet which had a shower with water piped from a mountain stream.

In the olden days many beach houses often had no electricity or running water - there were no building regulations then either, especially in very rural areas and Palmiet was one of these homes. As a result, odd rooms and passages had been built on as and when the need arose.

Lying in bed at night there, with the surf pounding the beach with a candle or oil lamp providing the only light is one of my abiding memories as a young child.

A key was available to get into the main house (which was heavily shuttered from inside when empty) through an outside room. In one corner of this room was a very small trapdoor, built into the wall at ground level. Because of its size and position it was usually the job of a small child to go

Palmiet – Early Days

through this and once inside the main house they could navigate their way in the dark, shuttered interior to the front stoep, remove the bolted inside shutters to let everyone in.

One of the problems was refrigeration. My father had built a wooden frame and covered it with wire netting, which contained lumps of charcoal. This would be kept constantly wet, and the air flowing over it provided a cool atmosphere for milk and vegetables mostly. Later we had a paraffin fridge which operated off a flame burner and that fridge was deliciously cold. The outside safe was also kept going as we caught a lot of fish.

The men and boys would walk what seemed like miles, but was in reality around half a mile, along the beach to the Palmiet River lagoon where seine nets were set to catch harders which came in to the lagoon at high tide from the sea. A harder (also known as a bokkom) is a Southern Mullet which is caught and braaied or dried and salted. This delicacy grows to around 40.5 cm. It tasted delicious on the fish braai (bbq). In those days we also had abalone (perlemoen), mussels, octopus and other seafood in plentiful supply to keep us going. My mother would make seaweed jelly using the yellow fronds found on kelp (seebamboes in Afrikaans) which were then dried. I recently found one of her recipes for this which I have appended at the end of this story for those interested – it is definitely an acquired taste! The nets would then be cleaned and hung out to dry on milkwood trees next to the house.

The house itself was surrounded by thick bush and milkwood trees and wild camphor with vygies (mesembryanthemums – a member of the aizoaceae family it has a long-lasting flower head and is found in more arid or coastal regions) abounding. There were many spiders, snakes and sometimes baboons visiting at close quarters. The ground had clusters of triple- pointed thorns scattered from thorn trees and walking barefoot was always a problem.

The big house was a haven of tranquility. One part of the stoep was known as 'old folks' corner' where the adults used to gather – and was also a resting place for Readers' Digests of yore going back many years. I remember the most uncomfortable ancient chairs being in old folks' corner – probably to discourage young children from sitting there!

Palmiet – Early Days

Next to the Red House (100 yards or so distant) is another house with a silver roof, also originally built with some of the Gustav Adolf's ship's timbers. This was an Albertyn family home. (This was burned down on July 10 1997 by three teenagers but has since been rebuilt). In a newspaper article 'The Wrecked Barque' of 1 July 1902 it makes mention of the seven survivors housed in Kleinmond by Mr. Albertyn who lived there. The Luckhoff's were related to the Albertyn's going way back and both family groups still get together often to this day. Nowadays Charlotte Swart who is in her mid-nineties lives there on and off with Marelise her daughter, and are often visited by her children Werner, Pieter and Charlotte and Marelise. Such a close-knit family who always make one feel welcome. They look after the Red House now as few of the Luckhoff's seldom visit it.

We used to visit Palmiet on weekends and spend the school holidays there as we lived quite close by in Worcester Cape, about 68 miles (110 km) distant. After moving to Rhodesia in 1958 my Dad would drive the 1,500 miles from Salisbury (now Harare) to Kleinmond towing a caravan – and park it up under the milkwood trees – some of us camping, others staying in the Kalfie cottage. Usually we tried to spend some of the summer months at Palmiet. Family members would come from all over South Africa to get together. On the day after New Year there would be a religious gathering of the clan at 'Die Stroompie' – a little stream – on a relative's property near De Wet's Bay a few miles away. There were always plenty of church ministers who were family members who had their say! We had a strong sense of belonging and equally strong family ties that continue to this day.

Seaweed Jelly Recipe from my mother Isabeau Luckhoff Granger as she wrote it.

'The seaweed is always attached to brown bamboo (sea kelp). The bamboo is wet and shiny when fresh, but black, hard and brittle when dry. The seaweed suitable for jelly is wine-coloured or pink and white fronds found on the bamboo. Collect from 4-5 pieces of bamboo with seaweed – it should be dry bamboo – if it is still wet, leave it in the sun for several days to dry. Then wash well in sea water to remove all dirt and sand. Then cut the seaweed from the bamboo and wash thoroughly under running tap water. Then place the seaweed in a fairly large saucepan and cover with tap water. Boil for around half an hour slowly.

Palmiet – Early Days

Strain into a bowl and to this strained water add the juice of one lemon, a few cloves, one cup sugar, one wine glass of wine (optional). Allow to set.'

Note that you do this at your own risk!

3

Helga Giving Me Sex Education

I admit it – I was a late starter when it came to this sex business. Boys and then teenagers in Rhodesia in the 60's were too busy catching snakes, collecting birds' eggs and shooting with pellet guns to be bothered with girls. There was some interest I know from the early starters, especially at class birthday parties, where everyone was invited, none of this selective friend business that one finds nowadays. We could play 'spin the bottle' and hope for the best. Here you sat around in a circle – boy, girl, boy girl – and the lucky one (or terrified one depending on how you looked at it) would spin a coke bottle and where the long end pointed that particular girl would have to give you a snog. Don't get me wrong, I am sure many enjoyed it and it probably led to marriage on more than one occasion, and it was definitely a taster for an eleven year- old for things to come later.

Helga Giving Me Sex Education

My two best friends Nigel Vaughan and Barrie Green and I had been discussing how unprepared we were should a girl actually offer us some attention and wanted IT!! Egged on by suggestive poses in Scope and Personality magazine (girl draped over beach ball eating ice cream; chap in tuxedo with Black Magic chocolates making massive inroads into woman's attention through offering her one), we knew we had to get the knowledge. The older boys were such braggarts, one thought they were at it night and day, and we were assured our turn would come soon. I guess we were age 11 going on 12 at the time. All three of us were scouts (5th Marlborough), and 'Be Prepared' was our motto.

The bottom line was that we had to get hold of an 'FL' or French letter as Durex or condoms were known as in those days. The girl would insist we wore one to avoid pregnancy, otherwise it was a no- go area.

We had also been told, on exceptionally good authority, that if you didn't want to embarrass yourself by asking the lady in the chemist shop for a pack of FL's, all you had to do was stand at the counter and flick a two and six coin (50 pence today) up in the air and bang it down on the counter, and she would know instantly what it meant and dispense the product accordingly, without any fuss.

So, the three of us pooled our pocket money and rode off to Marlborough Pharmacy in Salisbury (now Harare) on our bikes. Once there, we drew straws to see who would be volunteered to go in and make this life-changing purchase of a packet of three – one each!

It was me – my heart sank. A boy with a stammer going in for the confrontation with the pharmacy woman – (whom we knew was familiar with all our families) and I was much too young to be even thinking of getting prepared for the big day. I just prayed it would be the young chap who worked in there as an assistant and not the old harridan who you knew would tell your parents.

As the queue got shorter it was finally my turn and there she was in front of me, piercing blue eyes, with just a hint of inquisitiveness. Neck wrinkled I notice. OMG I had forgotten what they (the FL's) were called! Nothing daunted I flicked the two and six coin and brought it down on the counter. She just looked at me. I thought she probably didn't see it, so did it again. Again the stare. Man behind me in the queue (who knew my father) says stop playing games, boy, we are in a hurry.

She says 'Well, what do you want?'

In desperation I toss the coin up again and it hits the counter – maybe she will get the message now. Nothing doing.

'Make up your mind kid and stop wasting time – there's a long queue behind you' she says.

The coin flipping strategy is definitely not working. The man behind says get a move on.

I say 'That comb, a bar of soap and a razor please'.

She takes the money and gives me a few coins change. I get out of that pharmacy as fast as my legs could carry me.

The chaps are outside waiting to divide the spoils. Nothing like expecting your first condom and ending up with a comb or a bar of soap instead. 'But we gave you all of our pocket money' says one. 'Better wait until next week then' retorts I. Next week, the coffers are replenished and off we go again – this time a hard cycle ride to Mount Pleasant Pharmacy. I go in again. I get the young guy and flick the two and six coin – he knows instantly what it is, and says 'Small, Medium or Large?' He could have said 'Tiny, Big, Extra

Very Big' and I wouldn't have had a clue. He then says, 'Smooth, Ribbed, Extra Phlanges'. This was a new one on me. I turn around looking for inspiration from my friends who are nowhere to be seen – having seen Mrs. Mckenzie, our next - door neighbour, pop in for a box of tissues and some eye liner.

I knew I had to make a quick decision and go for Medium no Ribs to be on the safe side.

Outside the Pharmacy, we open the packet and each take one. Just in case.

Some thirty years later, I found an old wallet long disposed of in a desk drawer, and there it was, the 'just in case' condom. Now crumbly with age, it disappeared in a cloud of dust when I opened the previously sealed strip it was in. Of course, it wasn't sealed as I had taken it out to look at it and slipped it back into its packaging when I first got it. So yes, we knew we had to take precautions, and were well prepared. We didn't really progress matters much until we became Six Formers in High School.

That was when I met Helga for the first time. Helga was Swedish (and no doubt still is), and our Headmaster at Sinoia High School, Rhodesia (now Zimbabwe), Mr. Talbot-

Helga Giving Me Sex Education

Evans, a fine Welsh educationalist, introduced her to me. Thinking we required some sex education before we left school, the Headmaster arranged for a sex education film to be shown to us in Current Affairs at Sinoia High School which traumatised me for ever. Helga was later advertised in Illustrated Life Rhodesia in April 1969 as 'The First Sex Education Film' (in Eastman Colour), and told the intimate story of a young girl going through the following:

- The conception
- The fertilization
- The Birth
- The Sexual problems

and

Important – Patrons are warned that this colour film contains scenes of an actual birth and may be unsuitable for certain younger members of the public. In the opinion of the Rainbow Theatre Management. 'Helga' should be seen by all children over the age of 12. However, we would advise parents to see it first to make up their own minds on this point.

Blondie Requited

We had to watch the actual birth which was agonising to say the least!! One could say that the girls watching were squirming in their seats and 100% of them were sitting cross-legged – no hope of any future action in the short term from any of them – and as for the boys, well we were fairly open-mouthed throughout as we watched the terrible story of screaming Helga giving birth. Enough to put you off for life. Shirley Trickett (nee Cumming), who had already left school, saw the film said 'I saw the movie in Salisbury and went into labour with my first daughter the following night!' Graham Brand, an old boy, who was later in the same squad as me in the BSAP, said that his late mom made all three of her sons go and see it and was far thinking for doing so.

That film was the extent of our sex education when at school. Most felt that self sex-education was a better bet, and bragging seemed to play a large part. For example, the fact that a lad in your hostel could carry at least 6 wet towels on his erect appendage without dropping one was a feat in itself. Stumbling onto a copulating couple in the long jump pit when bunking out to cook a few mealies (maize cobs – corn on the cob) in the field next door was another.

Helga Giving Me Sex Education

Nowadays sex education is given to five-year olds in school, and people are much more aware of the do's and don'ts in relation to sex.

4

Taking the Body to Soweto

In 1971 I was a student at Rhodes University in Grahamstown, South Africa. Not any old student one might say, but an entrepreneurial one. In other words, Pater's stipend having dried up due to non - performance at the end of the first year, (I had been forced to double up in my second year to repeat the first year), and funding the lifestyle required taking on paying jobs.

At the time I was night manager at the Settlers Inn Motel, which also required occasional bar work and which was owned and run by Bertie Leach. The one thing about tending bars is that you get to meet some strange and interesting people. One such fellow was the area manager for a weather coating house exterior painting outfit that was currently blitzing every village in the area, including the town of Port Alfred on the coast some 35 miles away. All houses were painted a brilliant shade of white, and it was apparent that the special offers being given to house owners were having the desired effect in generating new sales. The company had divided its workforce into teams and the teams in the Port Alfred area were led by a young fellow who hailed from Soweto, named Jacob. I think he was of Zulu extraction, but his family had moved to the Johannesburg area many years ago to work on the mines.

Named after Queen Victoria's son Prince Alfred whilst on a visit to the area in 1860, Port Alfred was an 1820 settlement established as a buffer between the Cape Colony and the Xhosa people. It was originally named Port Kowie for west bank dwellers and Port Frances for those living on the east bank, until these amalgamated in 1860. It always has been and still is very much a holiday town. I nearly drowned there in 1978, but that is another story.

Young Jacob had been partaking of a few ales in a local shebeen bar on the outskirts of the town, when he was involved in a fight with a Xhosa man and sadly stabbed to death. His area manager was called out to the incident and related the story to me whilst enjoying a few snorts in the Settlers Inn Motel bar.

'You must understand Tony, I am needed down here to manage the team and have the problem of transporting the body back to his family in Soweto', he said, topping up his brandy and coke. 'There is just no way I have the time to do it.' I said –'easy – just get a local funeral service to make the arrangements'. 'I have tried that' he replied 'but they won't go that far'. The distance from Port Alfred to Johannesburg is over 1,000 kilometres - a very long way by road.

He then asked me if I would do it. He was to provide the transport (VW flatbed truck) and we settled on a price of R500 plus petrol costs. The truck with the coffin in the back was to be delivered to me the next day.

To put things into context, Soweto was not a place frequented by white people in the 1970's, and with South Africa's draconian apartheid laws, if a non-black person was discovered there it was a criminal offence. I had never been there before, but the media impressed upon us that it was an extremely violent place and the hotbed of political agitation against the South African Government at the time. So, taking a deceased African home to his family in Soweto was not without its possible dangerous consequences.

Taking the Body to Soweto

I fortunately bumped into my university friend Sholto Douglas, who was partaking of tea and cakes on the lawns outside Phelps house at Rhodes University in Grahamstown (where I was a student – apart from the hotel work I was also doing), and asked him if he would like to go on an excursion to Johannesburg for a day or two. Sholto was, and still is, a larger than life character, tall, with a beard and charisma that attracted no end of ladies. His problem was a constant lack of the folding stuff and an almost total reliance on his mother for cash handouts. Things were so bad that to save petrol he would freewheel his old green Opel down hills to save fuel. Also, being an Oppidan, he lived at home and not in university halls of residence, and when wanting to impress his girlfriend brought her out the farm I was living on for some Manhood training. I figured he would be good company on the forthcoming trip.

The promise of R50 (in today's terms around R750) for his trouble sealed the deal. I was to pick him up the next morning at School House, Kingswood College, where his father was Housemaster and the family lived. I duly arrived and parked the truck with the coffin on the flatbed outside the dining room window and went in for breakfast. During breakfast, his mother Edna enquired of her boy what he was planning to do today.

'Oh just going to Jo'burg with Tony, Ma' responds her son in all innocence. 'What for?' retorts Edna. 'Just taking a stiff to Soweto says he'. 'Ha Ha, don't joke, you should be going to lectures', replies Edna looking out of the dining room window and seeing the truck with coffin for the first time.

This was a woman you did not cross in a hurry. Telling Sholto in no uncertain terms he was going nowhere but to the Rhodes University campus, she made a beeline for the telephone to call every judge and magistrate she knew to get one or more of them to stop him from going.

'Let's get out of here' says Sholto, 'she will have the cops on us next!'

So, we bolted, jumped into the truck and headed out of town as quickly as we could. The journey was a long one and we picked up a number of hitch-hikers en route, some of them sitting on the coffin not realising what it was – until Sholto told them – hasty exits at the next stop as not many people relished travelling with the dead body for company.

Taking the Body to Soweto

We had no maps of Soweto, only an address. Soweto means 'SOuth WEstern TOwnships' - the name given in 1963 to the collection of black African townships to the southwest of Johannesburg. On arrival we asked for directions a number of times and were soon driving more and more into the centre of it, through thousands of makeshift huts and houses, along unmade roads and paths. We didn't see one policeman or Government official and were as nervous as hell. Eventually we found their road and located the house of Jacob's mother and sisters. I got out and approached the door with apprehension and knocked on it. His mother answered and astonished to see a white man called out, and her daughters came running. I explained that we had brought Jacob home. 'But where is he?' asked his mother. Then it dawned on us no one had informed his family of the death, let alone that he was being brought home. This unexpected turn of events produced much loud wailing, and before long a crowd of hundreds of people gathered around the truck and coffin, with much pointing and gesticulating towards us. Sholto managed to calm them down and explained the position, and how we had taken great risks to bring the body home to them.

We were invited in for tea and experienced great hospitality. A guide was provided to navigate us out of Soweto and back onto the highway and we headed back to Grahamstown in record time. Needless to say, I was persona non grata in the Douglas household for many years after that. However, I can honestly say the trip was an incredible experience.

Right - The house my grandfather built from ship-wrecked timbers – Aunt Charlotte and Tony in front.

Left - The beach and sea in front of the Palmiet House- Lovers Walk path.

Right - Tony, Debbie, Angy, Isabeau Granger – Marlborough, Salisbury 1962.

Left - Denis Granger and his son Patrol Officer Tony Granger BSAP 1974.

Right - Tony Granger after his pass-out. Morris Depot, Salisbury 1974.

Right - In front S/SO Jannie Steenkamp (instructor), Commissioner Sherren, David Smith MP reviewing squad 7/73. Visible lined up POs White, Spiers, Clancy, Hagan (best recruit), Edwards, Granger 1974.

Left - Police Commissioner Bristow presenting Tony (the new recruit) the BSAP 'Blue and Old Gold' book.
Recruited as a regular after Rhodes University and told 'Three years in the BSAP is better than a degree'.

Right - South African Police (SAP) reservist, Claremont, Cape Town, South Africa 1982. (Known as Konstabel Granger die Rooinek Engelsman –the Redneck Englishman).

Above - Tony Granger marries Joy Benson 30 April 1977.

Above - Sons Chris and James Granger at Nicola Granger's wedding in the South of France.

Right - James Louise Chris Anna Tony at Chris and Louise's wedding August 2020.

Left - Debbie Alvord Tony Granger Angy Cozens – me and my sisters USA March 2018.

5

Hitching a Ride

Hitch - hiking or thumbing a lift from motorists was one way of getting around when I was a student in the early 70s – you stood on the roadside and held up your thumb and hoped that a car, or any vehicle in fact, would stop and give you a lift. Danger did not enter your thinking (as a reason not to do it), and it was just great fun. Not that anyone would do it today – the only hitch hiker I have seen in the last 10 years in the UK was a chap in the motor trade hitching a ride to collect a car – easily discernible by the number plates carried under his arm. Of course, I stopped the car and he hopped in – he had hitched from East Sussex and was heading to pick up a car in Oswestry, a journey of some 250 miles. He was 73 and said he loved cadging lifts from people.

Blondie Requited

Graham Bursey had been at school with me at Sinoia High School in Rhodesia (now Chinoyi Zimbabwe) and we were in the same class. Graham was from farming stock, and his parents farmed in the Banket area of Rhodesia. Naughty from the tips of his toes to the top of his head, he was continuously in trouble both at home and at school. Nicknamed 'Hoekoe' (meaning chicken or fowl) this came about because one day he sneaked out of his hostel at school with a .22 pistol and made for the African police residential quarters at the rear of the school. There he knew that plenty of delicious chickens were available for the picking. After bagging at least two fowl he headed back to Stuart House just in time for roll call before the evening meal, the two now very dead chickens tied around his neck with bootlaces and tucked in under his blazer. Dick Meech, the duty master, ever perceptive, noticed blood dripping onto Graham's shoes and trickling on to the floor. Unperturbed due to Hoekoe's endless mischief and escapades, he enquired politely whether he was ill or injured as follows:

'Bursey what the bloody hell are you bleeding all over my floor for?'

Hitching a Ride

Hoekoe, ever fearful of any recriminations arising from (1) having a pistol in his possession and (2) what the African police sergeant would do to him once the crime was discovered, went into immediate cover-up mode.

'Nothing Sir, just a nose bleed'

'Not bloody likely' said Meech, opening up Hoekoe's blazer to discover the two plump chickens happily dripping blood on to the floor. Hoekoe immediately confessed to this crime saying he never had enough to eat at school and was thinking of supplementing his diet with some fresh meat.

'Six of the best for you and then over to the police quarters to explain to them what you have done'. The police sergeant was not amused to say the least and threatened all sorts of punishment. In the end Hoekoe had to pay double compensation for his loss, which enraged his father who ultimately had to pay for it. The .22 pistol was confiscated, but nothing more was said about that.

Graham thought he could put his past behind him when he went to Rhodes University in Grahamstown, South Africa to read pharmacy. Unfortunately for him, I also turned up at Rhodes University and knew his background. Subsequently he later read law and became a magistrate and advocate and author of six books about his life called 'SILF' *(Sweet Innocent Little Farmboy)*. However, I digress.

In 1970 as first year students, Graham and I decided to hitch hike to Cape Town to sell university Rag magazines during our vacation. Rag was a charitable institution and produced a magazine of fun, jokes and games which was sold countrywide to produce funds for the local poor and various other projects and we students were 'encouraged' to do our bit. Each armed with a box of magazines we hit the road and two days later made it to Cape Town – some 12 lifts or rides later. Our first night was spent sleeping under a road culvert near Port Elizabeth's drive - in cinema – that night we climbed a tree alongside the drive-in to watch the movie from afar, along with twenty -odd locals who also couldn't afford to get in to the outdoors cinema. There was no sound (as the movie's sound was only piped into the cars at the drive-in) but we had a bird's eye view of the movie in the distance. I think the movie was 'A Man Called Horse'.

I had taken off my jeans and boots before climbing into my sleeping bag under the road culvert where we bedded down

Hitching a Ride

for the night and woke up in the morning to find both boots and jeans frozen stiff – it would have been fun watching our comical endeavours to get dressed! Our next night was spent at Wilderness on the Garden Route to Cape Town. We could see a hotel about half a mile away on a hillside. This turned out to be the Fairy Knowe Hotel – described nowadays as the 'old dame' and is beloved throughout South Africa as she was the honeymoon destination of choice in her heyday! With history dating back as far as 1874 one can only imagine the splendour of days gone by. Situated on the banks of the Touw River, the hotel forms part of the Wilderness Nature Reserve and Estuary. Wilderness is one of only five documented areas in the world that has, within a five - kilometre radius, sea, land, rivers, lakes and mountain ranges.

I suggested 'let's cut across the veld instead of taking the road to the hotel – as it will be shorter. I thought we would save a couple of miles at least and as there was no chance of cars were stopping to give us a lift at that time of night. The going was heavy and getting more and more swampy and the Rag magazines were getting heavier and heavier. Just short of the hotel we stumbled onto the Touw river which we hadn't seen from the road. Having no alternative – in we went and managed to wade across. Being students, we didn't have much money, but we managed to persuade the night manager to let us sleep in an alcove off the lounge. He bought a few magazines from us which paid for our breakfast.

Eventually we arrived in Cape Town and stayed with friends in one of the University of Cape Town residences. Once there we managed to sell some of our Rag Mags, which was a relief. Graham had made a name for himself when he visited one of the female residences to sell our Rag Mags, when a group of Amazon - like female students cornered him and bundled him into a laundry basket, telling him he would be ransomed for their own Rag funds. This did not bode at all well for him. Meanwhile I was busy selling magazines at another University of Cape Town residence and did not know what had happened to him. Eventually I found him and bought his excuse that he had no alternative but to give his share of the Rag Mag money as ransom. So penniless, after a few days we decided to head back to Grahamstown.

Hitching a Ride

On the way back we managed to hitch - hike as far as Caledon, some 70 miles (113 Km) from Cape Town, where we then stood for many hours, cars and lorries passing endlessly and no one stopping. Eventually, some seven hours later, an old VW Kombi stopped and offered us a lift, which we gratefully accepted and we climbed in the back of the vehicle where the couple's young daughter was nursing a year-old infant. The driver seemed pleased to see us and offered us a swig from the ginger brandy bottle from which he was drinking whilst driving. Graham and I looked at each other and must have had the same thoughts. The more we could drink, the less he would drink we thought hopefully, and the bottle of ginger brandy was passed backwards and forwards between us until it was finished.

'No problem' remarked the driver 'I have another bottle here' – he produced said bottle and pulled the cork out with his teeth. 'Would you chaps like some more?'

Well - I had had more than enough and was 'on my ear' so to speak. The drink was vile and although I was feeling ill, I was considering whether to help the driver out or not when Graham kindly took the bottle and held on to it. The driver by this time was more than merry and was now swerving the VW Kombi into the path of oncoming traffic as he reached back to retrieve his now confiscated bottle of ginger brandy. For the past four to five miles we had been trying to persuade the driver to stop and let us out, but he had other ideas and kept demanding his bottle back whilst continuing to drive erratically. Luckily, fate stepped in, in the form of a traffic policeman, who then intervened and directed the vehicle to the side of the road. Had he not done so I am sure that we would have ended in a terrible accident. The driver was arrested for drunk driving, all the while protesting his innocence, whilst alleging we had given him the booze!

Graham and I were arrested for travelling in the same space as a non-white person, as the driver's daughter and her child were classified as Coloureds under the ridiculous apartheid laws in force at that time. We spent the night in the cells at Riviersonderend (literally translated as River without End in Afrikaans), and hit the road as soon as we were released. It took me a further three days to get back to Grahamstown, some five hundred miles (800 Km) away, whilst Graham was picked up by a local farmer who drove to a nearby airfield and flew him back home in a couple of hours, as he said he needed the flying hours!

Hitching a Ride

Even though I owned a car at University, as students we were always short of money, so hitch-hiking or begging lifts became a rite of passage if you wanted to go anywhere without payment. I had been discussing taking a holiday break with my friend Rob Humphreys, a fellow Rhodesian student from Salisbury, and we decided to travel to the Granger family holiday cottage Palmiet, near Kleinmond in the Western Cape for the Easter break. We had picked up a ride from a lovely elderly lady just outside Port Elizabeth – she was driving to Gordons Bay where she lived (only about 25 miles from where we were headed), which was perfect. She was happy for the company and asked if we would share the driving with her, which we did. Any hitch-hiker will tell you that to get the best lift or ride is one that takes you as close to door to door as possible. We still had well over 400 miles to drive and would manage the trip in a day which was fantastic.

When we arrived at Gordons Bay she asked if we would like to see her boat. We didn't know that she owned a boat, as it had not been mentioned on the trip down. 'Sure' I said 'I would love to see your boat' as she parked up at the marina. There at anchor lay a 42- foot beautiful single hull yacht which she said was hers. She told us that her husband had owned it for coastal sailing trips but had passed away about a year previously and as she was not keen on sailing she wanted to get rid of it. None of her family wanted it either. Rob and I looked the yacht over and it seemed to be in great condition and well maintained. Not that we knew much about yachts.

Then came the bombshell. 'I want you two boys to have the yacht'….'Whaat' I gasped – 'we know nothing about yachts let alone sailing them, (whilst thinking it might be a good way to get back to Grahamstown via Port Alfred after our holiday weekend). She offered to give us the yacht and didn't seem to think our non-sailing ability would hold us back. I told her the yacht must be worth hundreds of thousands of Rands and she just couldn't give it away to two students she had only just met. I said there was no way we could accept her yacht as a gift, but that I could put her in touch with my uncle in Cape Town and did a lot of sailing who could try and sell it for her. Eventually she agreed to this and I think was relieved as she evidently was looking for a way to get rid of it, without being ripped off. We stayed at her house in Gordon's Bay that night and the next morning I made arrangements for the disposal of the yacht. She then offered to drive us to Palmiet, near Kleinmond, to our holiday home, some 50 Km distant, which we gladly accepted. The only thing I remember about that weekend stay was finding an old can of condensed milk and boiling it for a pudding! Also, much fishing was involved. It took us nearly three days to hitch back to Grahamstown, but we had a great Easter holiday and nearly owned a yacht!

Years later, during my second stint at Rhodes University, and after a short career in the British South Africa Police in Rhodesia, my wife Joy and I were living in a house in Bertram Street in Grahamstown, which was opposite the police station. My friend Ian 'Tubs' Walker was going back to Rhodesia for the holidays having cadged a lift off someone. He collared me in the street outside the Vic pub where I was walking my dog Blondie and asked if I would look after his car whilst he was away. 'Just leave it outside your house' he said, 'and give it a run from time to time to keep the battery charged'. The car was a battered old Renault R4 with the gear stick in the dashboard. Many older readers will remember them well, I'm sure. Off Tubs went on his holiday for a month (he had some sort of running job for the Bookies at Borrowdale Race Track in Salisbury) and I promptly forgot about his chariot parked in the road outside my house. About two days before his return, my wife Joy, as sharp as a pin, said 'Shouldn't we give Tubs' car a run to charge the battery?' 'Good idea – 'let's take the fishing rods and drive up to Port Alfred, spend the day there and motor back – that should put plenty of vuma (power) into Tubs's battery''.

The Renault R4 took a while to start, but eventually it did. All set to go having loaded up two dogs in the back seat and my wife Joy in front with supplies and fishing rod. We first stopped for fuel and then headed out towards Port Alfred at the coast – a distance of 57 Km. We'd be there in no time at all I thought. About 5 Km short of Bathurst (about 30 Km from Grahamstown) the car made one of those moaning followed by groaning noises as the engine seized and it came to a shuddering stop at the side of the road. I immediately checked the battery – Tubs would be happy as it was fully charged, I thought. My wife went into the 'I told you not to take his car, now look what's happened' mode – forgetting she had suggested it in the first place.

Hitching a Ride

After sitting in the car for a full five minutes I got out and extended my thumb and the first motorist passing took me to Bathurst where I could use the pub's telephone to call for a tow to Grahamstown. That was the last time I ever hitch-hiked. Tubs on his return was adamant that I should pay for his whole repair, as the engine seizing had happened on my watch, and I was responsible for it. Turned out the car lacked oil (the oil guage wasn't working) which led to its heart attack – to keep the peace we eventually settled on me paying half the repair bill.

6

BSAP Patrols – My First Station

I attested into the British South Africa Police force in Rhodesia (now Zimbabwe) on 18 December 1973 at the not so tender age of 22, following a recruitment campaign for regular policemen. I was Patrol Officer 9086 and in a squad of 28 young men. Having completed my degree in economics and law at Rhodes University, I thought of joining as a regular as opposed to being a national serviceman, where continuous call-up was operating – at least I would have the benefit of being paid for my efforts! The recruiting officer Fred Mason made a PR event out of my joining as I had a degree, and Commissioner Bristow presented me with the Blue and Old Gold book on the BSAP. The recruiting campaign ran with 'Here's someone who thinks 3 years in the BSAP is better than having a university degree! '. Once I had finished my training in Morris Depot based in Salisbury, I was offered a staff job on promotion but opted for being a district policeman instead.

BSAP Patrols – My First Station

The police force was divided into Town and District policing in the main, with specialist units inbetween, such as the paramilitary Police Support Unit.

In my squad 7/73 were four other young men from Sinoia High school where I had been a pupil – however they were fresh out of school and a lot younger and obviously fitter. The school was situated some 65 miles from Salisbury (Harare) on the road to Kariba and Zambia. Many of the scholars were from solid farming stock and were well-honed in bushcraft and tracking. As a result, with the bush war in full swing at that time, a number of boys joined the armed services when they left school – in fact I read somewhere that there were more Sinoia High boys in the SAS than any other school, which is some going and quite an achievement.

My squad had the pleasure of doing equitation instead of PT, but we had to get up in the early hours of the morning (whereas the PT squads were up a bit later) to groom our horses and ride out. All of us squaddies had a 'batman' whose job it was to wash and iron your kit and make sure your boots, saddle and bridleware were well polished and shining. My batman was named Severino and I shared him with Steve Hagan, later to be 'Best Recruit' on passing out. We were issued with one or more horses, and my horse was called Utah – a massive brown stallion around 18 hands high with a nasty bite. When lined up on parade with our horses, more often than not, I would be next to Peter Allen whose horse Ukraine could wind its neck into a half circle and bite your leg if you were not careful. To pacify him (the horse not Peter) I would slip him a few mint imperials which he had a penchant for – when the ride got going Peter's horse would breathe a cloud of menthol into the air which was a great surprise to our instructor Inspector John Pearce. Peter Allen and Andy Loubser thought they would have a bit of fun the night before pass-out and 'borrowed' two horses from the stable lines and set off across the cricket pitch at Morris Depot. Peter was swept off his horse by a cricket stay holding up the sight screens on the edge of the cricket field and ended up in the camp hospital, his horse making it back to the stables safely where the piquet guard found him and then discovered another horse was missing. Andy spent some time in the guardhouse for his trouble. The latter now makes his living through writing successful crime novels!

BSAP Patrols – My First Station

After driving school I was posted to my first choice police station which was Inyanga, (now called Nyanga) joined by Danie Freeke also from my depot squad. The drive from Salisbury (Harare) is 165 miles by road and I drove up in my VW Kombi with my two spaniels, Blondie and Dagwood. Inyanga is situated in a lovely part of the country, the Eastern Highlands, in Manicaland Province, where the lakes and pine forests and misty hills are reminiscent of Scotland according to some. Inyanga is a popular tourist resort, with mountain trails, trout fishing and golf courses.

To the south lay the city of Umtali (now Mutare) about 70 miles away and to the north was an escarpment which dropped down some 900 metres to an area known as Inyanga North. When I was posted there it was known as Inyanga, although now it is Nyanga and I will use both names, depending on what it was then, and is now. The highest mountain in Zimbabwe is Mount Inyangani, which lies about 12 miles southeast of the town, and its highest peak is 2,600 metres (8,500 ft) above sea level. The highest waterfalls in Zimbabwe, the Mtarazi Falls cascading from top to bottom at 760 metres (2,490 ft) are also to be found in the region.

Historically, it's outstanding beauty prompted Cecil Rhodes to write to his agent in in 1896 saying *'Dear McDonald, Inyanga is much finer than you described .... Before it is all gone, buy me quickly up to 100,000 acres and be sure to take in the Pungwe Falls. I would like to try sheep and apple growing'.*

Inyanga Police station had a complement of an Inspector – John Collier the member in charge, and two section officers, Jon Milner and Ken Budd as well as half a dozen patrol officers, including two national servicemen, Fred Hammond and Stuart Comberbatch. The latter were well known for standing close to the burning piles of cannabis (mbanje) brought into the police station for destruction following court cases. The aroma used to hang over the area for days. There was also a special branch Inspector Jerry Cleland, a former Federation national boxing champion, and as tough as nails. The balance of the police contingent was AP – African Police, led by a police sergeant-major.

My first posting occurred the next day, following my arrival at Inyanga. I had met up with the police station officers and their families at the Rhodes Inyanga club on the Sunday (before I started work on the Monday) and was invited to play in a badminton match with John Collier who was the member in charge, Jon Milner, Duncan Stewart and myself. I had never played badminton before and John Collier kindly had me on his side of the net as his partner. When it was my time to serve, I did a classic miss-hit, the shuttlecock shooting off to the left and hitting John straight in the eye! He was none too pleased and had to go to hospital to have his eye attended to. The next day I was called in to his office, where he sat behind his desk with a bandage around his head, covering his eye. He announced he had had enough of me already and was posting me to Ruangwe to set up a police post and base there.

The area was gaining attention because of infiltration of guerrilla groups from Mozambique intent on subverting the local population, and it was felt necessary to show a police presence to reassure the locals. Ruangwe lies approximately 100 miles north of Inyanga, on the A14 road to Nyamapanda and a new Police base had been surveyed on top of a hill in the area. Close by are two church mission stations, Regina Coeli a Catholic one, and Elim Mission, a Protestant one. Both had schools and were no doubt vying with each other for converts. A large number of school children had been abducted by terrorists to go for terrorist training and this was of great concern to the Government. Whilst still in the Inyanga police area, Ruangwe scenery was nothing like Inyanga. There were no pine forests or trout streams with clear flowing water. Instead the bush was more like the lowveld, arid scrub-like, and much hotter. If lucky, one may catch a barbel or a carp in the Gairezi River which formed the border with Mozambique, only a few miles away.

Our small police contingent was housed in canvas tents and I had slung a hammock between two trees so I could gaze over the valleys below me when in idle mode. In no time at all I had established a tented charge office and mess tent, a shower cubicle made from reeds with hot water piped from a 44 gallon drum with a fire lit beneath it, a long drop loo and accommodation tents for the staff. Any prisoners held for criminal offences, as well as witnesses for court cases were housed under a big tree in the open air. After my time there, I heard that more permanent structures had been built at Ruangwe complete with bunkers to provide shelter when the base was mortared or attacked.

BSAP Patrols – My First Station

My initial patrols were to both the mission stations. Not a friendly welcome was to be had at either of them, as they were deeply reticent about showing any friendliness towards the Police. We knew that this was because of terrorist infiltration in the area and had intelligence that the mission stations were regularly visited by them. However, I did play chess with both Father Regan and Father Egan at Regina Coeli on the odd visit there, whilst my accompanying constables sought intelligence on the ground. The Elim Pentacostal Mission was in a similar position and did not welcome any police presence. They were another part of the Elim missionary group that were slaughtered by ZANLA terrorists in the Vumba on 23 June 1978 where 9 adults and 4 children were bayonetted or axed to death. We often used to ambush the paths leading to these mission stations in the hope of finding a terrorist group on the move and were successful on more than one occasion.

Ruangwe was where I experienced my first murder investigation and arrest of the guilty party. A young woman whose husband was away working on the mines in South Africa, had given birth to a little boy (the father not being her husband). As her husband had been away for the past two years, and was sending money back to her kraal to support her, she clearly did not want to be found with a young infant when he returned, so quickly decided to strangle the child and bury him in an ant - bear hole nearby. Her father who was the kraalhead, had an extremely strong sense of justice, and walked some 60 miles to the police post to report the death and the murder. If he had not done so, we would never have known about it. My sergeant and I drove him back to his kraal in my police Land Rover and questioned his daughter, Regina, as to the facts of the matter. She readily confessed and indicated the ant - bear hole where her son was buried. I prepared the case and typed up the docket on the old Imperial manual typewriter taken with me to Ruangwe, and managed to follow it through, other duties permitting. She pleaded temporary insanity in mitigation to the murder charge and was sentenced to 5 years in prison.

Another incident was when I was en route to conduct enquiries for the CID in Salisbury (Harare) at a kraal about 30 miles away from the Police Post, to locate an accused, who was wanted for housebreaking and theft. His fingerprints had been found at a housebreaking and I had been tasked with doing a home visit and arrest him if possible. Travelling on a dirt road with a bus in front of you belching black smoke and kicking up dust is not a pleasant experience. It was a typical African bus loaded to the gunnels with people inside and mountains of goods, bicycles and chickens in coops balanced precariously on the roof. There is no way you can overtake as you cannot see beyond the bus because of the dust cloud enveloping the dirt road. I was therefore surprised when the bus stopped in the middle of the road and the driver got out and approached the police Land Rover (he must have seen me behind him). 'Ishe' (sir) he said ' there is a woman about to have a baby on the bus – can you help?' The woman was carried off the bus by four passengers – each holding either an arm or a leg. My sergeant quickly dropped the tailgate of the Land Rover and she was rather unceremoniously placed on the bed of the vehicle, whereupon she commenced advanced labour and I knew that delivering the baby was imminent. Instant panic. No hot water, no towels, no baby extraction instruments! I had completed a St Johns First Aid course whilst in Morris Depot and all I remembered was that the umbilical cord had to be cut – but how? I forgot anything I had ever learned about babies and had never thought I would need to be a midwife. Fortunately, we had reasonable radio reception where we had stopped and I quickly called Inyanga Police station to be patched through to the hospital. The duty officer's wife was a nurse and she was in the police station at the time on radio duty and quick as a flash came on air to assist. The baby was almost ready to arrive and I had to be prepared. We had a first aid kit in the Land Rover containing a pair of scissors and bandages and of course mercurochrome (the red dyed 'muti' used for all ailments from cuts and bruises to wounds). Heave ho and out the baby came head- first thankfully so no breech. I wrapped the baby in the sergeant's blanket and tied off the umbilical cord in two parts and cut it in the middle as instructed. I wiped the baby as clean as I could with water from our water bottles and handed it over to mother. After some ten minutes the mother said thank you, got up and walked off to get back on the bus, which had waited for her. I thought 'yes well if it was my wife (not that I had one then) she would have spent at least a week in bed!'.

BSAP Patrols – My First Station

To the east of Ruangwe was the Nymaropa farming area which bordered Mozambique. The border was the Gairezi River, which in the dry season at that point, one could almost leap across, it was so narrow. The Government had invested extensively into a model farm development scheme complete with irrigation in the area, where new farming methods were taught to locals. The village of Nyamaropa hosted a bottle store where ice cold beer was served. One could observe Frelimo troops on the other side of the river from its verandah and their close proximity did not bode well for the future.

I was happy to be recalled back to Inyanga police station after a couple of months at Ruangwe, and heavily loaded up with kit plus my dogs and batman Aaron, we set off up the escarpment to the land of pine forests and cold clear streams, ready for a good session in the Body Box, the police pub, which was close to the single quarters where I had a room.

En route back along the A 14 road towards Inyanga Village, I passed the base of World's View Mountain and noticed a number of cars stopped along the road, the occupants staring up at World's View. Situated on the escarpment of the Inyanga Downs plateau in the **Eastern Highlands** mountain range, just north of **Inyanga**, **World's View** is situated at an altitude of 2,248 metres (7,375 ft) with a 600 metres (2,000 ft) drop to the plain below on the western side. The viewpoint is just outside the northern edge of the **Inyanga National Park** and can be reached via an 11 km track from **Troutbeck Inn**. On a clear day, places as far away as 60 to 70 km can be seen. I stopped too and got the binoculars out to see what was going on. The occupants of the car next to me told me that a man was going to hang glide off World's View - the first time that this would be done - and that the press was there recording it. As we watched, the hang glider took off and was hurled back into the cliff face by the wind, crashing into the rock and the pilot dropped some 300 feet on to a rocky outcrop to his instant death. As the only police officer at the scene, I radioed it in. The upshot was that the Air Force had to send a helicopter out to recover the body from the mountainside. It was estimated that almost every bone in his body was broken during that fall. Apparently, he had been told not to fly as the wind conditions were not right, however went ahead regardless as the press were already there to record

BSAP Patrols – My First Station

it. I recovered the body from the Air Force helicopter and drove to the Police Station to do the paperwork and to open an SDD – a sudden death docket. Whilst working on this, the recently - deceased's wife came in to see me, obviously in a very distressed state, shouting at me as if it was somehow my fault. I managed to calm her down – tea does help.

7

The Last Foot Patrol

I wasn't long back at Inyanga Police Station following my posting to Ruangwe when I had a call-out to a stock theft on the Kwaraguza Road between Rhodes Hotel and Troutbeck Inn. Old Colonel Wyrley-Birch lived up there and farmed sheep. He was a real character and ex Indian Army – always a delight to visit him and listen to his stories. On this occasion I took Fred Hammond, the national service patrol officer with me and one of the constables and the three of us set off in foul wet weather for the farm. On arrival, we were offered a cup of tea, which was welcome, and we settled back into the Colonel's comfortable sofas which were dotted around his large lounge. The Colonel brought us up to date on the stock theft. Apparently, half a dozen of his sheep had been driven off in the direction of Mozambique which was not far from his farm.

The Last Foot Patrol

Whilst catching up, I could see NSPO Fred fingering the anti-macassar skin on the back of his sofa - they covered the backs of all the sofas and some chairs. After a while, his curiosity got the better of him and he asked the Colonel what animal skin it was. 'Oh, that's old Rover – we had him skinned after he died from snakebite – was really quite fond of him you know'. NSPO Fred just sat there open-mouthed after this elucidating piece of information whilst I watched him closely to guage his reaction. 'And the others?' I asked tentatively. It was explained that each rug was a skinned family pet by which time we were shaken rigid!

Getting back to the business in hand, the Colonel indicated where the sheep had been and were now no more. Unfortunately, the rain had now obliterated all tracks, so the investigation was temporarily called off and the constable was detailed to make some local enquiries.

Our trip back was precarious, the track was wet and slippery and visibility was poor, and it was now getting dark and raining heavily. Breasting the brow of a small hill, the Land Rover began to slide sideways and no amount of corrective driving action could save us as it rolled over a couple of times, landing on its wheels. Thankfully, we were all right, albeit a bit shaken. The side wings were scratched and dented and a mudguard had to be straightened before we could get going again. The alignment of the Land Rover however was squiff and there was a massive steering pull to the right. I parked it up back at base and went to bed. A not a very happy member in charge discovered the modified Land Rover the next morning at vehicle inspection. 'Granger you are barely back here after injuring me (I had hit him in the eye with a shuttle cock at badminton) and now one of my Land Rovers is out of action. 'I think a long foot patrol will be in order for you'.

I was briefed to travel from Inyanga up towards Mount Inyangani and then down to the tea estates, which were in the Honde Valley near Mozambique. I was accompanied by Constable Wiri for company and interpreting duties. No horse, no bicycle, no Land Rover, just two pairs of feet. We set off from Inyanga Police station with rucksacks and carried weapons as we were heading into an area where there may be terrorist activity. One Greener shotgun and one FN – the shotgun for shooting for the pot should we put a partridge or guinea fowl to flight. The plan was to visit as many kraals and homesteads as possible, mainly to show a police presence and also to gather valuable intelligence on the ground   Hopefully accommodation would be found along the way, and this certainly turned out to be the case, as people were pleased to see us and liked to catch up on the news, as homesteads were few and far apart.

Customarily travelling by road from Inyanga Police Station to the Honde Valley the distance would be around 80 kilometres, travelling south on what is now the A14 through Juliasdale and the Inyanga National Park, then on the A15 to the Honde Valley.via the Pungwe Falls. This would generally take around an hour and a half by car. However, as we were walking, I planned to take a much shorter route, by cutting out the dogleg the road took further south. We would go directly east around Inyangani Mountain, ultimately making for Aberfoyle tea estate, and then on to the police post at Ruda where police transport would be sent to pick us up.

This fertile Honde valley lies 900m above sea level and was one of the major tea producing areas of Rhodesia. Aberfoyle Lodge, formerly the tea planters' club house, nestles in the hills among forest and acres and acres of tea plantations. Katiyo, Rumbizi. Chiwira and Eastern Highlands Tea Estates are among those situated in the valley, along with Aberfoyle. The descent from the highlands into the valley is awe - inspiring as are the waterfalls that cascade off the escarpment 700 metres above the valley floor. Mtarazi Falls is the most impressive and highest of these - with water coming from Inyanga and flowing into the Honde River. Muchururu Falls is fairly close to the Mtarazi Falls – both spectacular and ensuring a plentiful supply of water for those living in the hot valley below. To a lesser extent, coffee is also grown in the Honde and the valley also provides land for a number of subsistence farmers.

We spent four days hiking east visiting settlements along the way whilst revelling in the grandeur of the Inyanga National Park, and its vast pine forests and lush shrubs. We skirted Mount Inyangani and began the descent down into the Honde Valley. On arrival at Aberfoyle Tea Estates, the farm manager told me he was holding two tea - cutters who had been in a fight when drunk over a woman and wanted them charged with GBH (grievous bodily harm) for using their tea - cutting knives on each other. The local district nurse had patched them up and, at first glance, they

The Last Foot Patrol

didn't appear too badly injured. Those tea cutting blades are razor sharp and can cause a lot of damage, and on closer examination they certainly did. Whilst having a drink with the Manager and enjoying the sunset from his verandah (we were going to spend the night at his lodge), a telephone call came through for me from Inyanga Police station. Our only contact was by telephone as we did not carry a radio, however we had left our proposed travel itinerary with the member in charge back at base so that he would have a rough idea of where we were.

He told me that he had received an exhumation order from a magistrate in Umtali to exhume a female's body who had allegedly been poisoned. The kraal where the woman lived was about 30 km away, going south towards Umtali. As I was the only policeman in the general area, I was to attend to it in the morning. A Land Rover would be sent from Inyanga Police station to collect constable Wiri and me from Aberfoyle. So ended the last foot patrol for many a year in that area, as increasing terrorist incursions were making normal policing difficult to maintain.

Blondie Requited

The following morning, a Saturday, after a hearty breakfast (full English we would call it in the UK!), Sergeant Musa arrived with a Land Rover and body box to collect us. We were to locate and exhume the body and then take it to Umtali for forensic examination. The only problem was that I also had the two prisoners, charged with GBH, and they sat on the back of the Land Rover. The vehicle was not enclosed in the back and was an open flat- bed type. I borrowed a pick and two shovels from Aberfoyle and we set off for the grid reference we had been given. The kraal in question was on the side of a gomo (hill) and was a reasonably large settlement with some 40 thatched huts and a couple of brick dwellings. On arrival there, in seconds almost the Land Rover was surrounded by at least 50 people, all shouting at once, demanding to know our business. Most of the men were dressed in flowing white robes with a belt holding a sheath for a knife, but no knives were visible. They were part of an Apostolic Faith Church sect called the **Johanne Marange Apostolic Church.**

The founding of the Johanne Marange Apostolic Church in Zimbabwe can be traced back to the 1930s. It is one of the largest African Independent Churches with largely African adherents, blending local traditions with Christianity, with a focus on a ministry of healing. The church was founded and named after its founder, Johanne Marange in 1932. The founder was born in 1912 and died in 1963 in Marange tribal area and his parents were descendants from African royal families.

The church maintains strict obligations for the Sabbath day, or Saturday, and members are not allowed to work on that day. They also do not handle money on Saturdays nor do they allow members to cook on the Sabbath day. This is in line with the Jewish sabbatical laws in the Bible. The use of alcoholic beverages and smoking cigarettes are prohibited, as they believe these substances defile the body. Another obligation of the church is that members dress in long white garments for church services. Symbolically, it represents purity, light and cleanliness. They do not wear anything black in colour. Both men and women are head shaved as a sign of religious commitment to God. This Church accommodates and promotes polygamy. Johanne Marange as the founder of this social movement, had thirteen wives. This church has been promoting polygamy, and polygamous marriage, in line with traditional African as well as ancient Jewish cultural traditions. (*I acknowledge Julius Musevenzi Department of Sociology, University of Zimbabwe, Mt. Pleasant Harare. acrobat@sociologist.com and his article for this information*).

I called for the kraalhead and asked him to show us where the graveyard was and point out the grave where the allegedly poisoned victim was buried. He flatly refused to assist us and became menacing, as did the crowd. I tried to calm them down and asked the sergeant and constable to question some of the crowd privately, which they did – whilst I was forced to confront the mob with the Greener Shotgun. This confrontational attitude was not what I was expecting at all. Eventually the Sergeant returned and said a young boy would indicate the grave site, which was the grave of his aunt.

I explained to those present that I had an exhumation order from the Magistrate and I was going to do my duty whether they liked it or not. This was where the two prisoners from the Aberfoyle tea estate came in handy. Giving each one a shovel, I indicated where to dig. This was a most unusual grave site. The top layer was one of rocks, then soil.

The Last Foot Patrol

Beneath the soil was a layer of grain. Another layer contained the deceased's pots and pans and then another layer of soil. Beneath that layer was a layer of clothing and personal possessions. Then another layer of soil. The woman had been buried 6 months earlier and the putrid death stench was overwhelming. I had been sprinkling Jeyes Fluid (which we found in the Land Rover) on the grave diggers as they dug, just to make things a bit more bearable for them. Eventually amidst much cursing the two grave diggers stated they had reached the bottom of the grave and there was nothing there!

This conundrum posed a real challenge – the body had to be there somewhere. Indeed, it was – a shelf had been dug into the side of the grave right at the base. The body was concealed there, wrapped in a white robe, with a hard earth cement-like substance to hold it in place. The deceased was lifted out of the grave and placed in the body box. This repository was aluminium and very durable and once the lid was secured it thankfully lessened the smell. However, the vile fetor of death had permeated our clothing and was not very pleasant. At this stage, the two grave diggers were pleading that this was not how they usually spent their

Blondie Requited

Saturday afternoons, and begged to be let go as they considered they had served their punishment. I concurred that helping us was punishment enough, and they would be released from our custody when we arrived at the main road and they could walk home.

I then had to drive down to Umtali morgue to drop off the body. However, it was Saturday and unfortunately it was closed. I left the sergeant and constable at the African police camp and went to the single quarters, known as Silver Oaks at Umtali Police station, only to find it was full and that there was no accommodation for me. I then remembered my squad mate Steve Hagan had said that if ever in Umtali I would always be welcome to stay at his folks' place. I managed to find their house and parked up outside, then went to the front door and knocked. I could hear a conversation on the other side of the door, and then 'who is it?'

I replied that I was a friend of their son Steve and wondered if I could spend the night as I didn't have any available accommodation. The next thing the front door was barely opened and a bin liner was thrust through the gap. No doubt the stench of decayed flesh was more penetrating than I had thought!

'Take off all of your clothes and put them in this bin liner' which I did, now standing outside shivering. And then 'Put on this dressing gown – your clothes should be burned'. Oh no I thought – my only uniform can't go up in smoke! I was ushered straight through to the bathroom for a shower whilst the uniform visited the washing machine. The Hagans very kindly invited me to supper and asked me to relate the story to them about the morgue being shut. 'So where is the body now?' enquired Mrs. Hagan. On the back of the Land Rover I told them. 'In our drive ……..outside our house?' squeaked Mrs. Hagan totally aghast. 'Oh yes – outside the dining room window in fact' I responded. The upshot was I had to move the Land Rover up the road so it, with the vile-smelling coffin, was parked outside someone else's house.

The next morning, I dropped the body off at the morgue for the autopsy – I had arranged for it to be opened on the Sunday – and awaited the results of the post - mortem. The determination was that she had definitely been poisoned, and now began the search for the person who had murdered her. Apparently, the deceased's husband had taken another wife and she expressed her strong displeasure in no uncertain terms, and made her feelings known to him. His response was simply to poison her, then telling those in the village she had fallen ill and died suddenly. There were no mitigating circumstances with this one and he was sentenced to death for murder. I was disappointed that the foot patrol had come to an abrupt end, however, did have some adventures along the way!

Right - Tony posing on police Land Rover - Inyanga North 1974.

Left - Tony relaxing in the Ruangwe BSA Police post charge office, Inyanga North 1974.

Right - Setting up the BSAP camp at Ruangwe, Inyanga North – tents to begin with, it became more permanent later.

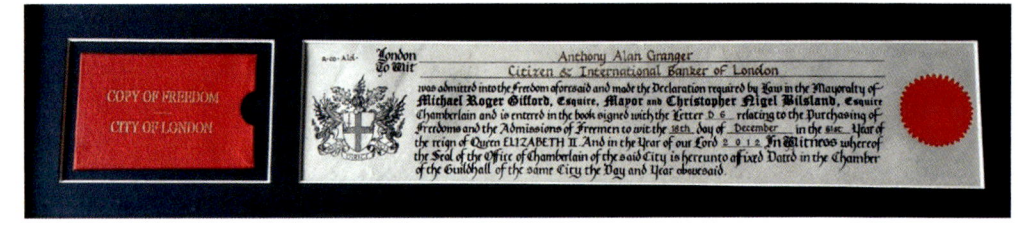

Above - Freedom of City of London 18 December 2012 through Worshipful Company Of International Bankers (WCIB).

Right - Tony exercising his right as a Freeman of the City of London to shepherd sheep across London Bridge without a toll being paid- 2017.

Left - The sheep in question were supplied by the Worshipful Company of Woolmen.

Right - Budgies Players Skene, Mickey, Case, Tony, World Golden Oldies Cardiff 2016 at Cardiff Arms Park.

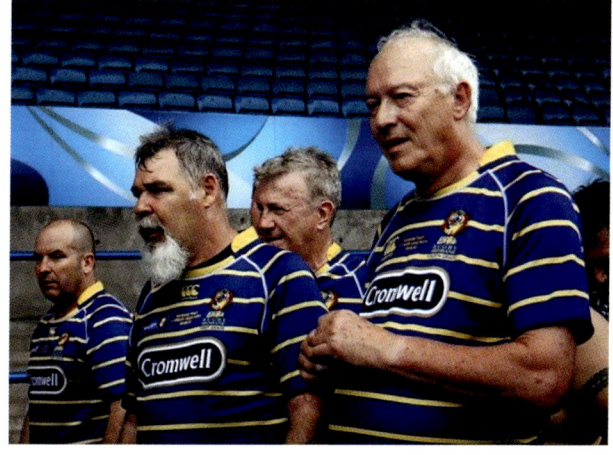

Above - Peter Drabble (UK) Tony Granger (UK) Geoffrey 'Gull' Phillips (Australia) Lew Aitken (Australia) World Golden Oldies Sydney 2010.

Above - Guinness World Record largest rugby scrum participant Cardiff World Rugby Festival 2016.

Right - Brisbane Budgies 2012 Fukuoka Japan- Tony Granger bottom row 1st left in Rhodesian rugby jersey.

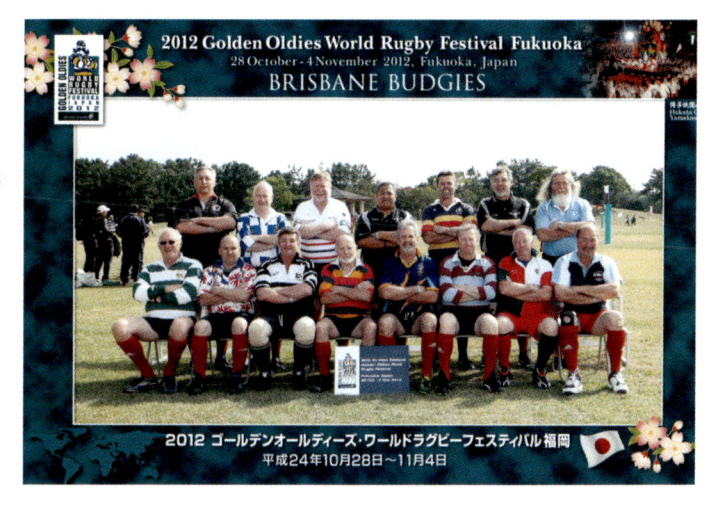

Above - Brothers Edgar Vincent and Denis Granger who signed up in South Africa on the day WW2 was declared.

Right - My father Major Denis Rhodes Granger in 2 Brigade Rhodesian army 1970.

8

Marrying a Known Terrorist

I had met Joy Benson at a braai (BBQ) given at our police officers' mess named 'Camelot' in Baines Avenue, Salisbury (now Harare) one hot Sunday afternoon in late 1976. Eight of us lived there – me, Alan Ledger, Mike Crabtree, John Sutton and his wife Sue, Alastair Kennedy, Mike Jones and Barrie Green. Only Barrie was non BSAP (British South Africa Police), being in the Air Force, and an old pal from junior school. The house was a rambling old Rhodesian - style ranch house which had previously been a nursing home named St. David's. My room was an old ward that had housed six elderly patients, and the other rooms were equally as big. There were domestic quarters at the rear of the house where my batman Aaron resided along with other batmen and cooks. We had a bar, based on the honour system, regularly well stocked with booze purchased from the Farmers' Co - Op. Beer cost us 11 cents a bottle in those days.

The grounds were impressive with rolling lawns, often covered with parachutes drying out after a day's skydiving, which was the pastime of some of the mess occupants. Most of us were either in the CID or Special Branch and it was unusual for everyone to be at 'home' at any one time, many of us being away in the bush on anti-terrorist or rural crime operations. When we were in residence, a side of beef or a sheep was purchased and a spit braai held on one of the lawns and our friends were invited with their families – sometimes as many as eighty people.

Joy was an English rose who had come out from Shropshire in England, after a few years of the Harold Wilson government, to see the world. She had applied to go to Canada where a friend of hers was working, but did not receive a satisfactory reply when a radiologist friend whom she had worked for at Royal Shrewsbury Hospital, contacted her and said 'come to Rhodesia – there's a radiographer's job going at Dr. Duffy & Muller in Salisbury, Rhodesia – and I can put in a good word for you'.

So off she went and before long made some very good friends. Two of those friends, Jan Walmesley and Paddy Krynauw, who worked with her, had husbands in the BSAP, and were invited to our Camelot braai and brought Joy along for an afternoon of festivities. That is how I met her and was immediately smitten.

At that time the Rhodesian bush war was in full swing and I had been posted to the North East of Rhodesia for long periods, with few trips back to Salisbury, but I made the most of them. My courtship included driving Joy up Dombashawa rock in a police Land Rover, almost vertical at times, and terrifying!; trips to Lake McIlwaine where I stranded us out in the lake by losing the oars on one occasion, and visits to my parents. Over nine months, I think I saw her five or six times. My dog Blondie did not take kindly to female opposition and began a regime of growling and nipping whenever she was near. Her favourite trick was to leopard crawl up the bed and get between the two of us, turn to me and give me licks, then turn to her and begin growling!

Then came the bombshell. Joy said that she was thinking of going back to England for her sister Jane's wedding and may not be coming back – unless...... we got married! That came as quite a shock to me as I had naively not considered it in my planning, and immediately thought of applying for more bush time. However, I was in love and proposed to her, selling my drum kit to buy the engagement ring.

Under section 2(1) of the Police (Marriage) Regulations, 1965 a serving officer had to make 'Application for Permission to Marry'. This was on Form BSAP 101. Application is made in terms of Standing Orders, Chapter 11, Section 32, 'Marriage of Members'. This application form was passed up the chain of command for eventual permission either given or declined by the Commissioner of Police. I submitted the form 101 on 18 January 1977, from my station at Special Branch, Bindura. It gave all the relevant particulars, including Joy's personal details. She had entered the country on 7 January 1976, met me and now we were due to be married on 30 April 1977 – I hardly knew her and we had only met up half a dozen times in total.

After waiting for about two weeks, I was called to PGHQ in Salisbury for a meeting with the Commissioner of Police, then Mr. Peter Sherren. I thought, 'wow', the Commissioner wants to personally congratulate me for my wonderful choice of wife.

I was marched into his office, and there he was with my Special Branch OC and various aides. He then began to question me.

'Where did you meet your intended wife?' he asked. I responded 'at a house party in Salisbury'. He retorted 'Are you sure it wasn't in Germany when you were on holiday in Europe in 1975?'

I replied no, it was definitely in Salisbury. He then said that the information he had from the Central Bureau Registry was such that I was lying and it was a very serious offence to give incorrect information. Naturally, I was flabbergasted and I objected in bewilderment that this could not possibly be!

The Commissioner then asked me if I knew that my intended was a notorious European terrorist. I replied that it could not possibly be. He then read from my 'Permission to Marry' form that Ulrike Meinhoff born on 7 October 1934 at

Oldenburg, Germany was my intended spouse. I said, no it was not, it was Joy Benson from Shropshire England.

Then the penny dropped – I had been sabotaged and set up – yet again. My form had been intercepted by my colleagues as it went up the chain of command and the spouse name changed from Joy Benson to Ulrike Meinhoff! She was part of the notorious Red Brigades faction that had been terrorising Germany for decades. (Ulrike Meinhof was arrested in 1972 and hanged herself in Stammheim prison during her trial in 1976).

To this day I don't know whether the Commissioner of Police was in on the joke or misdirection, but he certainly played his part well.

I knew it could only have been my colleagues Peter Dewe and Peter Stanton who were forever up to no good in the dirty tricks department. Naturally, they denied everything.

I was married in my parents' garden in Marlborough, Salisbury (now Harare) by the Chaplain General of the armed forces, Norman Woods, who later christened my sons in Cape Town. Terry Walmesley gave the bride away and Jan Walmesley and Annabel Lewis were bridesmaids –

Annabel being the then girlfriend Barrie Green who shared a house with me. John Jackson my best man and friend from Rhodes University gave the shortest wedding speech ever. Joy, my wife to be, looked absolutely stunning. My mother had organised the Vrouekring (Afrikaans for womens' group) to make delicious wedding food and her garden looked lovely.

I had been choppered in the night before, having been on ops for a few weeks, and managed to get rid of the beard before the big day. Staying at my parents' house, I was in the room next to the folks where I could hear them having a discussion – well it was more my mother having a go at my father, which went something like this:

'Denis you must tell him'

My father 'I'm sure he knows – he will have found out somewhere'.

This went on for a while. Finally, my father gave in and agreed to tell me first thing in the morning – the day of my wedding.

I lay awake thinking – what must he tell me? I must be adopted was the only thing that sprang to mind.

Next morning my father called me in to his study and said 'your mother and I have had a serious discussion and believe you need to know something'.

I asked him what that was, as I was expecting some real revelation.

'Well, you know about the birds and the bees' he began…

I said 'assume I know nothing'.

I then allowed my father to tell me all about procreation and I was 26 years old.

The wedding itself went off with a bang. Firstly, John Morris-Smith did his famous party trick and aimed his wheelchair at the swimming pool – this caused a number of well-dressed people to jump in to save him. John was an excellent swimmer and had a good laugh. My Triumph Spitfire was daubed with 'Just Married' paint which never came off. Joy and I flew to England for our honeymoon – she clutching the top layer of the wedding cake. Immigration admitted her through arrivals at Heathrow and she was in tears when I was detained for several hours before they allowed me in. It was all to do with my previous escapade (See Blondie's Revenge Ch 4 The Toy Soldiers). I had never met my in-laws before but had sent them a picture of my batman Aaron, saying it was me. I think there was a huge sigh of relief when they finally met me.

9

Children's Pets

My son James's first pet was a goldfish – only because I had won it in a fairground when visiting the 'knock the skittle off the shelf' stall, using a small beanbag. My throwing arm was good in those days. We bought a miniature aquarium and Goldie the goldfish was having a great time swimming around the little rocks and arches and sometimes pushing his wet lips up against the glass to see what's going on. James was responsible for his welfare, cleaning his fish tank, changing the water and feeding him fish flakes. One day I came home from work to find the little lad in tears. 'What's the matter son?' I said comforting him. 'I had cleaned out his fish tank and refilled it (the little fella gets scooped up in a net and placed in a glass of water whilst this goes on) before putting him back in to the water'. 'But he's floating upside down now and not swimming'. I told him not to worry and put my hand into the fish tank to retrieve the fish. No amount of police training ever dealt with fish resuscitation though. My hand shot out of the water as if an electric current had shocked it. The water was boiling hot! Poor James (not to mention the poor but now very deceased fish) had used hot instead of cold water to refill the fish tank. He then managed with a Syrian hamster to take his mind off aquatics, until that little beast unhappily passed away some months later.

My grandchildren now possess a hamster. It arrived today and is firmly ensconced in what looks like a Santa Grotto, munching away, storing food in those hamster cheeks. It reminds me of the time my wife Joy agreed to look after a friend's hamster named Rodney whilst they went on holiday. It had a secure cage and a hamster wheel for exercise. The little beast used to go round and round on that wheel night and day whilst practising to be an escapologist. One day it just disappeared! We hunted everywhere for the wee thing. I had no idea how it managed to get out and away and suspected the cage door may have been left open.

The day before our friends were due back, I bought another similar - looking hamster from the pet shop to replace the lost one, hoping they wouldn't notice. About a week later, we were having a chat with our friends who were discussing their now lethargic hamster who wasn't going demented on the wheel anymore and just lay there. In fact, when trying to stroke it, it gave a few sharp nips, totally uncharacteristic for their Rodney. Then it gave birth to a litter of baby hamsters which astounded them as they thought they had a male hamster! Well they did have a male one, but I wasn't to know this, and the one I replaced it with was evidently a female. Two months later we were moving some furniture around and, lo and behold, out popped a hamster from under the sofa which made a dash for the kitchen where I stopped it's escape. It had made a tidy home in the springs of the sofa and did look a bit thin!

Did I confess? No never – the obviously bisexual Rodney remains a total mystery to our friends.

10

Pofadder

Frikkie looked up from the mesmerising front of the tractor where the Mercedes bulls-eye had been his focus for the past six hours. The burning sun and heat had been forcing its presence down into the cab to mingle with the rising exhaust fumes and engine warmth. The sweat gunnelled down his back, rivulets of salty body water running down the inside of each of his thighs, soaking his balls. He shifted his weight to loosen his restrictive position, the crotch-part of his underpants digging deeper into the tender skin area. Whatever he did to ease things only seemed to be momentary.

He looked back through the dust and scarred thick plastic window at the miles of turned sods. Thick, rich loam, suitable for either tobacco or cotton, laid out in long straight lines behind him, the birds already pecking and scratching at the worms exposed by the scarrow. Arms, neck and legs, long browned by the African sun, had that sinewy cord-like quality associated with men of the soil. His eyes, rheumy from dust and middle-distance gazing, felt gritty and he subconsciously wiped his grimy hand across his face, leaving a sweat-streak through the dust and stubble. Switching off the engine, he jumped down to stretch his back and pushed the floppy cotton hat to the back of his head. Once white, it was now dirty brown with that reddish-ochre tint which never would wash out. Not that he had ever tried to do so, the hat being the standard uniform of all farmers in the area. He likened it to a Karate black belt, having read somewhere that Karate fighters started off with a white belt which was never washed. Over the years, accumulated grime and dirt gradually turned the belt blacker and blacker. He felt this experience keenly as he fought with the dry and arid soil every day of his working life.

His thoughts drifted to other matters. He hadn't had sex with a white woman for nearly six months now and could feel the familiar swelling bulge confronting the tightness of his rigidly-held crotch, which he adjusted again with both hands, pulling away at the restrictive garments under his pot-belly. The sun seemed relentless as he glanced swivel-eyed at it from below the floppy hat, and he knew that another six days of before dawn to after-dusk ploughing still lay in front of him. Bone-rattling tractor - shaking days with only hot air to breathe and even the drinking water warm. Not much to look forward to; no plans, no entertainment, nothing.

The last time he went out with Koos, Sarel and Pieter to Pofadder, the local town, they had really let their hair down, got blind drunk and ended up in chookie after breaking up a bar - no sympathy, but that was fun.

Everything was now so serious he thought. "Ever since the country was just handed over to the Blacks, Whites like us mean nothing anymore. Can you believe it, at the next farm a black man does the ploughing and he earns the same as me! It just isn't right. The Government has given away our birth-right without a fight", he thought. But his thoughts and inner arguments were tired, rehashed brandy and Coke confrontations with a past which was gone and a future of beans and chips. "Where is the steak?" he thought, "What a man needs is a good piece of red meat from time to time - that will keep him going!" This thought sat comfortably in his brain and, like a constricting tumour, his mind again drifted to a contemplation of his sex life and his needs. He must visit Johannesburg soon, he thought - after the ploughing. The decision made, Frikkie clambered back into the cab, released the cut-out and fired the motor to resume ploughing. The birds came out in greater numbers now, flocks landing to pull long juicy worms from the tightly encrusted earth surface behind the plough.

The tension had gone, no matter how confined the cab, no matter how the sun burned down its Summer message, Frikkie was happy. He sang, he laughed, he ploughed and ploughed. Furrow after furrow. Life had purpose he thought as he made his decision.

There was a lot to do to get organised. First to arrange a few days off, then buy some new clothes. Then to visit Oom Karel who wanted some money taken to his daughter who lived in Johannesburg, but whom Frikkie had never met. "Girls like Old Spice" thought Frikkie, as he adjusted his new cravat, tucked the ends into his safari suit and splashed on the cologne liberally.

Pofadder

He had a couple of addresses from Star magazine to arrange some fun - female fun. He would get settled first, then start visiting. This was his week and nothing was going to spoil his enjoyment of it. The car was a 1971 Mercedes and he slid in behind the wheel, tucking his belly in under the steering wheel and finding the pedals with his veldskoen. When he was far from Pofadder, none of those upright Calvinistic church - goers could have an inkling of what he was doing. These were Frikkie's thoughts as he powered the car Westwards, thrusting him closer to his objective. The more he thought about it, the more the images of release began to pound at his brain and speed up his heart rate. He pictured in his minds-eye the image of himself twenty years earlier making it with any number of beautiful women. Then he was slim, good-looking and solvent. The envy of other men who flashed courting glances at his many girls at the harvest festivals.

The next evening Frikkie went to the first of his addresses and asked for the girl by name. She came into his presence like a breath of lilac air - just like the air freshener hanging from his rear-view mirror in the car.

Katrina must have been about 23 years old and, although buxom in breast was slim-waisted and pleasant-faced.

"Good evening" said Frikkie appraising Katrina. She had lowered her eyes in the towering presence of this bronzed overweight farmer, to give an impression of coquetry, of shyness. She felt his awkwardness but had experienced this before and could easily deal with it.

"Is this your first trip to Johannesburg?' she asked. "No, I have been here before ₋ but a couple of years ago" he replied, again coolly appraising her body and those eyes fluttering, but not looking at him. Sudden panic flashed across his eyes as his tongue felt leaden and unresponsive. Small talk was difficult for him. Also, this woman had a reserve and a way about her which made him want her now. She sensed his inexperience and lack of present conversation and invited him up to her room, for she was used to these big, lumbering men, devoid of most social graces, who wished to empty their reservoirs at the earliest opportunity. Both knew what was wanted and had to be given and, as she turned and walked up the narrow stairs, he pulled off his hat and followed her docilely, like a dog.

Her room was large with prints of seascapes and wide-open plains, not unlike where he came from. Apart from the large old-fashioned bed, brocaded curtains with velveteen finish hung loosely against an open window, their hems draping on the floor of the room. A chest of drawers and couch with antimacassars draped over the back completed the furniture of the room. On the wall hung familiar looking photographs, of the kind found in any house amongst the farms where he came from. Frikkie felt at home.

"Shall we get down to business first, then we can enjoy ourselves?" asked Katrina, taking in the apprehensive tremors from Frikkie, whose last conquest was the black dairyman's daughter, which had cost him two rands. "O.K. how much is it then?" queried Frikkie. "Well, that depends on what you want" replied Katrina, "A hand-job is fifty rands and to spend the night is two hundred rands "

"It's no problem" responded Frikkie, "I want to spend the night with you" and, pulling out his wallet, gave her the two hundred rands. "For a beautiful woman like you, I would pay even more!"

Not even a premature ejaculation, which spurted his hot semen onto her stomach, a result of all the excitement and anticipation, could deter Frikkie, who rammed his point home again and again in self-interested gratification. Katrina lay there passively, sometimes moaning with pleasure, sometimes not, the insides of her body becoming sore with the persistent thrusting which showed no respite. As she was dreaming of home she was overcome by rising nausea occasioned by the intermingling of their sweat and the Old Spice's sickly sweet smell, she let Frikkie come inside her and quickly thrust him away , pulling up her legs so that her knees forced his withdrawal. She rolled onto her side and out of the bed, into the bathroom where she was sick.

By the time she returned, Frikkie had rolled onto his back where he was snoring, his beer gut rising and falling with his breathing. Katrina looked down and thought "I don't enjoy this but I need the money to survive." She caught the smell of his breath, foul, odorous, smelling of biltong combined with stale beer and cheap cigarettes.

Frikkie slept until just past dawn, when he awoke with the mother of all thirsts. "Poking is a thirsty business", he thought, as he padded to the bathroom and drank his fill. Returning to her bed, he gazed down at her still form and thought how beautiful she looked. And what a lover - she had moaned and groaned in ecstasy all the while they were doing it and really was enjoying herself. He could tell. "She must have thought I was fantastic" he mused as he contemplated his Adonis -like form in the semi-darkness and awakening of dawn.

Frikkie let her sleep and was content to think about the days ahead. They hadn't said very much to each other, but then he had been eager to immediately begin sexually pleasing her and, whilst he was doing so, there wasn't much to say. Today would be different. Having experienced what a great lover he was, he would allow her sufficient time to recover and they would have dinner together tonight. He had farming business to attend to, but also needed to replenish his toiletries, especially the Old Spice which seemed to do the trick with her, and which was running low.

That night, Frikkie came back to her apartment, which was shared with the other girls and again asked for Katrina. This time he felt and acted with a lot more self- confidence and she treated him with familiarity as opposed to the first night's coyness. She led him upstairs to her room and this time told him that he could stay, but for three hundred rands for the whole night. "Three hundred rands that's just about all I've got left. I was hoping to make it last a week" said Frikkie. "You have become special to me", said Katrina "and I want to give you a night to remember. Better a shorter, quality stay with me than wasting your money on unsatisfactory encounters".

Frikkie knew that she was taking him for every last cent but, so besotted was he, that he agreed to the terms. She did indeed live up to her promises and gave Frikkie a night to remember. As with the previous night, after he had thrust his final payload into her burning bush, she pushed him off and he rolled over, going to sleep immediately. Katrina lay there hating herself for what she had done and the tide of

Pofadder

nausea began forcing its way up from her craw into her throat. After she had finished with the bathroom, she crept back to bed and lay thinking of her family and childhood friends back home.

The next morning, Frikkie was up early and showered, ready to take on the world. Katrina saw him to the door.

"You know, we saw each other for two full days and I don't even know where you are from" Katrina said.

"I'm from Pofadder, where I have been a contract farm manager for a couple of years" said Frikkie.

"What a coincidence" said Katrina, "My parents farm is in the same area".

"I know" said Frikkie, "It was your father who asked me to give you the five hundred rands in the first place".

11

Helping Nelson Mandela Select his Jumble

I was working in Harrogate, a beautiful spa town in North Yorkshire in 1998 for a firm of independent financial advisers as their corporate development and professional connections manager, as well as being a financial adviser. My secretary Julie had a wicked sense of humour and we were continually playing tricks on each other – our office was a happy one, full of laughter. Julie's principal cohorts in mischief- making were Louise and Judith.

One day I received a letter from the SA Business Club based in London, of which I was a member, and similar to previous mail received in the past. It was an invitation to be part of a business leader group to escort South African leaders around London and I was allocated the President of South Africa, Nelson Mandela to be his escort. He became President of South Africa on 10 May 1994 and frequently visited London to give talks. I had previously met him at a function and was working with his office on how to

Helping Nelson Mandela Select his Jumble

regenerate small businesses in South Africa and was pleased to receive the invitation.

Quoting from the letter 'the meeting on Saturday 20th June will consist of visiting charity shops in the centre of London to get a feel of how much money is being supplied to the Third World at any given time. In order to appear inconspicuous, we suggest that you 'dress down' for this event, and your co-operation will be appreciated'.

I did some research and made a note of various charity shops and where they were. Julie then told me she had received a call from the SA Business Club to the effect that I was to focus on charity and jumble shops in Brixton and that arrangements should be made to collect items donated to South Africa. Also, that my wife Joy was included in the jumble shop tour.

I was very excited that I had been selected in this way and couldn't wait to tell Joy. We lived in Shropshire and I was a weekly commuter to Harrogate about two and a half hours away. The plan was to drive from Harrogate to Shrewsbury and then on to London on the Friday to be available for the historic tour of jumble and charity shops the next day with the President of South Africa. Joy no doubt visited local charity shops in Shrewsbury with her friends to get a feel of what could be donated and was asking me questions like ' how will the charitable donations in London be picked up and shipped to South Africa?' She also bought a new dress for the occasion.

The Friday duly arrived and I packed up my bags and headed for the car park to leave for home. As I opened the car door, I was immediately surrounded by around twenty people from the office who were clapping and laughing! I thought 'Wow what a send-off'! Julie then appeared from the crowd and gave me a 'You Have Been Had' card. I had been well and truly taken for a ride and had swallowed the bait hook line and sinker. Explaining it to my wife when I got home was no easy matter – 'Tony how could you be so gullible?' It still rings in my ears to this day as I remember it. Still she did get a new dress out of it.

A few months later I was going on holiday to our family holiday home at Palmiet, near Kleinmond in the Western Cape in South Africa. Before I left the office, the girls working there asked me to bring back some perfume from the duty free as that would make them extremely happy.

Helping Nelson Mandela Select his Jumble

Their happiness being my paramount concern I said I would be pleased to oblige.

A week or two into the holiday, whilst contemplating life on the beach, I decided to go fishing for Galjoen, which is easy to braai and delicious to eat. The Galjoen, coracinus capensis, is the national fish of South Africa. It is a species of marine fish that is found only along the coast of South Africa. This fish is found mostly in shallow water and is often in rough surf, close to the shore. It can assume different colours - near rocks the colour is almost completely black, whereas in sandy areas it is silver-bronze. The diet of the Galjoen is mainly red bait (ascidians), small mussels and barnacles.

For bait, one had to find a bait pod that attached to the sea bamboo or kelp, or it was found in rock pools, but often washed up onto the beach. The bait pod contains *Pyura stolonifera*, commonly known in South Africa as "red bait" (or "rooiaas" in Afrikaans). It is a sessile ascidian, or sea squirt, that lives in coastal waters attached to rocks or artificial structures. Sea squirts are named for their habit of squirting a stream of water from their exhalant siphons when touched at low tide.

Blondie Requited

The red bait is cut from the pod and either left to dry or can be used fresh. It has a stink attached to it that takes days to scrub off your fingers, and the fish absolutely love it. This gave me a brainwave of an idea. 'Rooiaas Perfume'! Dabbed behind the ears it will attract men like no other perfume. Absolutely ideal for the girls in the office. All of their boyfriend problems will be solved with just one dab.

I purchased some small bottles and had labels made describing the enticing nature of this wonderful eco-friendly man-attracter. I then placed a small piece of rooiaas into each bottle and mixed in some water. In a few days' time the putrid concoction would be just right to use and send the men delirious with desire.

After the holiday, I went back to work and there were Julie, Louise and Judith all waiting for the wonderful new eco-friendly South African perfume. I explained that once dabbed on it would last for days without having to be renewed. I offered to do the dabbing behind the ears, and although viewed with suspicion, all agreed and on went the rooiaas perfume. Well, within five minutes there was pandamonium as all hell broke loose with girls gagging from the pungent aroma now firmly embedded in eco-friendly

Helping Nelson Mandela Select his Jumble

manner behind their ears. Suffice to say it lasted for days, men were repelled and children ran for cover.

The score was now one all.

12

There's a Bomb Under My Pedals

In 1984 I was Manager of Old Mutual Financial Advisory Services (FAS) based in the Old Mutual Building on the corner of Darling and Parliament Streets in Cape Town, South Africa. The building was built between 1936 and 1940 and is a fine example of Art Deco architecture in South Africa, very much African inspired. It was for many years the tallest building in South Africa, and the Head Office of Old Mutual Life Assurance Society before it relocated to Pinelands. What I loved about it was that it had one of the longest granite friezes in the world, stretching along three sides of the building and depicting much of the history of South Africa at that time. Above the frieze are nine large native heads with tribal characteristics, each carved out of a six- ton block of granite. Inside the building, coming in through huge bronze doors, is a magnificent foyer, the walls covered by black and brown veined marble, and a ceiling of gold leaf.

There's a Bomb Under My Pedals

Walking into such magnificence every morning certainly set the scene for the day. I could feel the history flowing through the veins of this building. I ran a most successful sales operation with seven of Old Mutual's Top 25 salesmen in my branch. It was also the first true multi-racial branch of Old Mutual in South Africa, and my remit was to continue its success as the forerunner to the new South Africa which was going to come. Asked why I had been chosen for this position, the General Manager of Sales, Bobby Jooste, said 'Because you are a Rhodesian untainted with apartheid history'. To a certain extent this was true, as I had grown up in Rhodesia, but had been born in South Africa. My father, an attorney, had fought a number of constitutional cases on behalf of disenfranchised race groups, and his ethos of fair play and equality was imbued in his children.

On this one Friday morning I had driven into Cape Town in my light blue Toyota Cressida and parked in the multi-story car park a few blocks from my office. I managed to find a space on the 3rd floor and parked the car. I had a fairly busy day scheduled, my main appointment being to interview a prospective FAS member at one of our branches in the suburbs. I walked to the car park and took the stairs to the third floor, found my car, opened the door, and sat in the driver's seat. I moved my foot to depress the clutch as I commenced turning the ignition key and found that the pedal would not go down. I looked down between my legs and immediately saw a brown paper package with wires coming out of it rammed under the pedals. Immediately I stopped turning on the ignition as the thought 'Bomb' flashed through my mind, and that it could be activated by the ignition. It was dark in the car and I was focussed on nothing else but the package at my feet. My next thought was 'what if it's a pressure switch?' Getting out of the car could release the pressure and activate the bomb.

I made a decision. Opening the car door, I gently eased myself out and .....nothing happened. Relief swept over me like a tidal surge in a tsunami. However, the threat was still omni-present and I had to do something about it. Prior to my career in financial services I had been a detective in the British South Africa Police in Rhodesia (now Zimbabwe) and had some experience of explosives, but not very much. However, I recognised the threat – if the bomb went off in a multi-story car park it could collapse at least part of the structure and loss of life would certainly follow. I stopped the first person I saw walking towards her vehicle about ten spaces from mine and asked her to call the bomb squad. I then stood behind a pillar about twenty feet away and proceeded to stop pedestrians from coming into the area.

Within ten minutes the South African Police Bomb Squad arrived and swung into action as I told them the story. One of their number kitted out in padded clothing, a shield and visor then cautiously approached the car and swept the underneath for any explosives. He then approached the open door and bent over in the area where the package with wires was, eventually carefully bringing it out. Delicately he unwrapped the brown paper surrounding the bomb and exposed the wires trailing from it.

'Is this your cassette player?' He said, passing it me. I was still in a state of adrenalin-induced shock as I examined it. The relief swept over me with the realisation that someone was not trying to kill me. South Africa, at that time, was experiencing shootings and bombings as the nationalist groups pursued a military end to apartheid, and I was wondering whether I was a target, for whatever reason.

Someone had broken into my car and stolen the Pioneer radio system, also removing the tape player. The latter had been wrapped up in brown paper and rammed under my foot pedals. I had not noticed the missing cassette player nor the radio when I got into the car at all.

I duly reported the theft to the Police and to my insurers, Mutual and Federal. I was asked to take the car to a radio shop in Long Street to have a new radio and tape player fitted, which I duly did, leaving the motor vehicle at the radio installation workshop for the day.

I collected the car and the radio worked perfectly – it was one of the top -of -the range Pioneer systems and expensive to buy or replace if it was me doing it instead of the insurance company.

Two nights later my car was 'broken' into in my driveway in Claremont, and the radio stolen again. I could not believe it. The car was locked and there was no sign of forced entry. I reported it to the police and again made a claim on my insurance. I was asked to go to the same radio repair and installation workshop, which I did. The newly- fitted radio worked perfectly. I also found it strange that the technician had marked my favourite channel with a touch of permanent ink marker pen, just as I had done.

'Hello', I thought –'that's far too much of a coincidence'. I spoke to my contact at Mutual and Federal insurance and he said they were paying out a fortune for stolen radios and tape players – mostly stolen from cars more than once. Time for the detective hat to be worn. The police, incidentally, were still following up on enquiries and had not made any arrests. When I told them that the first radio stolen from me had been replaced in my vehicle following the second theft, they could not believe it.

It turned out that the radio repair and installation workshop used by the insurers were in cahoots with a gang of thieves. When your car went in for the new radio installation, an impression of your car key was taken and of course they had your address details. The second theft was as easy as pie.

13

50 Years of Rugby

I can honestly say I have played rugby for over 50 years, and in my latter years as I was much older wound down with what we call Golden Oldies Tours or veterans rugby, mostly to other countries. Initially I played rugby at Sinoia High School in Rhodesia, and because of my height, was positioned at lock or second row. My lock partner in those days was Bill Malkin, whose parents hailed from Kariba. Bill and his lovely wife Lynne live only about 40 miles away from me in Chester and we remain good friends to this day. We had an extremely good rugby team from under 14 upwards and were largely unbeaten. Our coach was history teacher Roy Gordon, who was passionate about rugby and it showed through us. One aspect I did not like was having to change or swap rugby jerseys during practice. One boy who had bursting acne all over his back always made a beeline for me when the instruction came to swap jerseys!

50 Years of Rugby

After school I played house rugby at University, followed by Villager Rugby Football Club in Cape Town when Joy and I moved there in 1980. Villagers had 14 open sides in those days and I managed to get as high as the Third XV. I was 29 years old then and hadn't touched a rugby ball for a while. We had moved to Cape Town from Grahamstown to join Old Mutual and being short of funds we needed a loan to get settled in. Tubby Teubes, who worked with me at Old Mutual was also Villager RFC Club Chairman and said he would arrange a loan through Barclays (the then Villager RFC Treasurer worked for Barclays) provided I turned out for the Club! Villager RFC is the second oldest rugby club in South Africa, established on 2 June 1876. I later served as club secretary for many years, and represented Western Province Clubs at the SARB, which entitled me to tickets at Newlands for the major matches. My father had played rugby and cricket for South African provincial sides in the 1930's, and his club was Gardens, having been a pupil at Wynberg Boys High School in Cape Town.

Whilst working as a detective in the British South Africa Police in Rhodesia (now Zimbabwe), Joy who was from

Blondie Requited

England and I were married in 1977 and we came over to the UK to stay with her parents on honeymoon. After meeting some of her friends who played rugby for Bishops Castle and Onny Valley RFC, (which is based in South Shropshire), I was invited to play in a match on a freezing cold winter's day, with snow on the ground. Having come straight from the Rhodesian bush where temperatures were in the 90's+, it was hard to adapt to the near freezing conditions. Not really up for it, I tried the old 'I don't have any boots' excuse. 'No matter' said Neil Phillips the team secretary 'I will get you some', and there I was playing on very hard ground making my English debut. Some 40 years later I am a Vice President (VP) supporter of Bishops Castle rugby club. This remains an extremely active and small club – for many years the pitch was, and still is, grazed by sheep and the clubhouse is a local pub. Grassroots rugby at its very best. Twice a year the VP's attend an excellent lunch put on by Sally Phillips and her team and then watch a game, cheering on the up and coming rugby generation. One memorable occasion was when I was playing in a particularly hard-fought match against a Birmingham team, known for its robust play and ended up in a punch-up with an opposing lock. The ref blew his whistle and gave them a penalty and sent me to the sin bin, sporting a black eye. A few days later I was due to meet with the Headmaster of the Wrekin school to discuss school fees planning for the parents, and to my astonishment there was the said referee cunningly disguised as the Head - Master! Fortunately, he had a sense of humour, and after a few comments about my black eye, got on with proceedings.

In the late 1990's I took over the mantle of English veterans' rugby manager from Jeff Butterfield who had played for England and the British Lions in the 1950's. He and his wife Barbara owned the Rugby Club and Restaurant in Hallam Street, London where I first met him. We were discussing Golden Oldies rugby, lamenting how few touring UK Golden Oldies teams there in fact were, and he asked if I would I be interested in forming a team, as he was retiring from management. I went back to Harrogate in North Yorkshire, where I was working at the time, and spoke to Patrick Finnegan, a work colleague, about forming a Golden Oldies touring rugby team. This resulted in the birth of The Full Monteys team- combining players from Yorkshire, Shropshire, Gloucestershire and Cheshire. In later tours

Vince Murphy took over from me as team manager, later to be succeeded by Richard Clegg on Vince's untimely death.

On our travels to different countries we often combined with the Toothless Tigers, a team from Brisbane and this later led to the formation of the Budgies as a touring team, which included players from six countries (Australia, New Zealand, Samoa, USA, England, South Africa), led by the able dentist Geoff (Gull) Phillips. My last game with the Budgies was at the world Golden Oldies rugby tournament in Cardiff in 2016, when I turned 65.

Where the New Zealand All Blacks had the Haka to inspire fear in their opponents, we had 'The Full Monteys welcomes you' (or words to that effect) painted in large black koki pen letters on each player's backside – each cheek would have a letter on it. This was fully presented to the opposing team to create an element of terror in them before each game. We would all line up facing the opposing team and then jig around to present them with the message. We joined the Air New Zealand Golden Oldies fraternity which hosted games in a different country every two years, and our first tour was to the world games in Cape Town in 1998. The only requirement was that you were aged over 35, and breathing, to play in the Golden Oldies! Shropshire stalwarts included Russell and Jo Jones, Peter and Zena Reynolds, Richard Rowlands, Bart Mallard, Dave (a ref) Joy my wife and me. Ian and Barbara Marsh (Lady Babs) joined from Gloucestershire, Vince Murphy from Winnington Park in Cheshire and Steve Manning from Australia. The Harrogate contingent included Patrick Finnegan and the 'Dangerous Brothers'. The two brothers (former British army parabats) became known as such because they took a dislike to the Argentinians who were billeted with us, even though the Falklands War had ended in 1982, some sixteen years previously. I had a devil of a job to keep the peace.

Our first game was against Northern Transvaal Jesters. We really didn't know what hit us – it was like a juggernaught rolling over us – yes, we lost! Our second game was played against the Orange Free State Morreesburg Farmers – men built like Arnold Schwarzenegger who carry mielie sacks (about 112 lbs) around for fun. We needed some tactical advantage here. Unbeknown to our opponents I had lived in South Africa and was fluent in Afrikaans, the language spoken by the opposing team. In the lineout if the hooker was throwing to number 3 he would say 'drie' meaning 3. I would then tell the forwards – 'it's going to number three' and so on. They just couldn't understand how we 'Engelsmanne' (Englishmen) had out-manoeuvred them at every turn. The game result was a draw. At the presentation afterwards we exchanged plaques and beer mugs and I addressed them in Afrikaans.

'Where did you learn our beautiful language?' asked their captain. I replied that 'I learned this speech especially for you and this game', whilst watching as tears rolled down the cheeks of those burley men amazed that an' Engelsman' could go to such trouble.

From our post- match report:

'....because it was held in SA, the South African teams were determined to win at all costs, whereas we were there for 'all the sport'. As Tony Granger (the tour manager) was fluent in Afrikaans, we managed to get all the line out calls in advance and he reduced the farmers to tears by addressing them in 'die taal' after the match. (They had previously reduced us to tears during the game!). The Monteys gave a magnificent display of their gloriously painted bottoms at the beginning and end of each match, which became the talk of the tournament, as did our 'bullshit deflectors' which were handed out in place of pins, and could be worn, one on each ear to deflect the most serious of non-rugby talk. It must be mentioned that both Dave Christensen and Bart Mallard played in a game against medical advice and have not been the same since!' Russell Jones, our amateur pilot, provided the highlight of the tour, when flying Vince Murphy and Pete Reynolds near Cape Point, by almost colliding with an Airbus, causing an instant requirement to repair to the pub. The tour culminated in the gala dinner when 6,000 people sat down to a five- course meal in a railway goods shed converted for the purpose.'

Our last game was at Green Point Stadium grounds. This was a truly traditional friendly game against the Silver Ferns, a local team playing in the true spirit of comradeship and fraternity. So much so that Steve Manning invited Martine, the daughter of a friend, onto the pitch for a run out. With the opposition bearing down on her (Steve was known as a non-tackling scrum half so was quick to dispose of the ball and had passed it to her), she instantly saw the danger and threw the ball up in the air and into the path of a traffic policeman on horseback along the side of the playing field. He caught the ball and galloped towards the opponents try line where he passed the ball back to her and she scored a try!

Cape Town had a number of firsts for our touring party. On the second day driving back to the hotel after a game we were delayed in traffic whilst the police had a shootout with a man on the run; and as mentioned before, Russell Jones our prop was a pilot back home and hired a small plane to take some of the team on a flight around the Cape peninsular – the next thing he knew he was flying alongside an Airbus coming in to land, and was no doubt given the finger and told to get out of the way. He then made a name for himself drinking more pints of beer in an hour than anyone else, a record that probably holds to this day.

In 1999 the Full Monteys headed for Adelaide, Australia, where we joined up with the Toothless Tigers from Brisbane. Our kit, had been impounded in Melbourne (as it was not used and considered new), however, the local rugby authorities pulled out all the stops and managed to get it to us in Adelaide half an hour before our first game. My rugby boots had been impounded in Perth on the flight into Australia, as good old English soil was found between the studs. The customs official took them and steam cleaned them for me, and it was a relief to get them back. At the welcoming parade where all the visiting teams parade on the first day, Vince Murphy disgraced himself with a full-on brown eye before the Premier of New South Wales, which was reported in the national press. Mike (Lappy) Lapworth and Stella found a traffic cop at the parade who in turn found their long lost cousin, also in the police force; Peter Drabble found a drunken Legless Emu and guided him for the next week, before stealing a taxi (complete with passengers) from the hotel. We played the Sydneysiders, the NZ Maoris and New South Wales teams and happily had a three- win scenario.

Each tour has its remarkable players, many coming with family members and unique events that are imprinted in one's memory forever. The organisation of the golden oldies' festival is immense, and the attractions laid on would not be available anywhere else. Some events cater for up to 6,000 players and supporters. For example, playing rugby in San Diego USA in 2005 was an event to remember. The rugby playing fields had been set up on the San Diego polo club fields and as you drive into the grounds huge signs shout out that this venue is sponsored by both Porsche and

Ferrari. Teams of polo ponies were being exercised everywhere around you. Our game was due to be played at 1 pm when the sun was at its highest – around 26 degrees centigrade. We were due to play against an Australian side and the scene was set for some action – but what transpired was not what we bargained for! On this tour I had taken my wife Joy, friends Tom and Frances Crichlow as supporters, and our son James, the latter as physio or massage man to the team and anyone else in the vicinity. James was 23 years old then, but a bit of beard and lack of hair made him look a lot older. He was desperate for a game, having come all that way with us and not to be involved was not on his agenda. The minimum age to play was 35, but we didn't think anyone would notice. James' main supporter, his mother, was on the side of the pitch under a sun umbrella, it being very hot and she needing shade. James received the ball on the wing from the Gull, Peter Drabble (Drabs) having made a magnificent dummy pass to get it to him, and made a run for the line, only to be tackled by two Aussies right in front of where Joy was standing. In her opinion (as a mother) she thought James was being unfairly tackled by these bigger blokes and began to lay into them with her umbrella! Good job everyone saw the funny side of this encounter.

The USA Golden Oldies farewell dinner was held on the flight deck of the USS Midway an aircraft carrier permanently docked in San Diego harbour. A five-course silver service dinner ensued with country and western singers entertaining us afterwards – what an experience. Later the team bought James a camera for his physio and massage work on them, which I thought was a great gesture.

In 2016 I found myself as a player at the World Golden Oldies rugby festival in Cardiff, Wales, playing for the Budgies, in what was to be my last game at the age of 65. The Budgies, although comprising mostly Australians from Brisbane, had 6 different nationalities playing for it, with players from the USA, South Africa, England, New Zealand, Samoa and Australia. Ably led by dentist and hardman Geoff Phillips known as 'Gull', we played four matches in five days, culminating in a final game on the famous Cardiff Arms Park ground, refereed by Nigel Owens of Wales, thought to be the best referee in the world. We won all of our matches which were mostly hard-fought but enjoyable.

Cardiff was special because I participated in the Guinness Book of Records world record for the largest rugby scrum comprising 1,297 players on 24 August 2016. The previous record of 1,198 was set at Twickenham during the Rugby World Cup. (Our record has since been beaten with 2,586 people taking part at an event organised by Young Entrepreneurs Group Toyota (Japan) in Toyota, Aichi, Japan, on 23 September 2018).

Welsh referee, Nigel Owens, also received a Guinness World Records award for refereeing the most international rugby matches.

Rugby has been a large part of my life, and I have played in many countries, including South Africa, Rhodesia, United Kingdom, Australia, New Zealand, USA, Ireland and Japan, enjoying every minute of it – it has given me much fun and many new friends!

14

Are Writers Philosophers?

Fourteen writers rode into town, pens at the ready, to record what they can.

Cologne, city of scents, our path along the Rhine, the road to the Markt der Chocolatiers was the first port of call. Willy Wonka was not there, but we filled our boots on chocolate delights. The sugar rush pointed the way back to the philosophical roots found in the coffee shops around Museum Ludwig and the magnificent Cathedral that centres Cologne.

Deep history and art, what does it conceal? The meeting of spies, the turn of the wheel – Birkenau and Auschwitz the gypsies' ordeal?

Every painter a philosopher every writer one too – from Cubism to Surrealism and Symbolism and other art forms, are writers not artists too?

Our thinking inspiration for writing our thoughts from that deep well of experience exploring our thinking as artists do. We think, we write, the artist thinks and paints a picture for all to see. Are our books not canvasses expressing our thoughts and deeper meanings as we twist and turn plot and word at every turn?

The Artist thinks and paints a picture for all to see – in full view for all with the price of admission. Our literary works may seldom be seen, but they are there and may find greatness in years to come. The 'now' of the Artist may stretch back thousands of years, our now is ever present, as we evolve our art form.

Our writing may seldom be seen and unlike the artist allowing others endless speculation on what is or might have been. We probe our core being for those very ideas to commit them for others to see, read and love us for what we have done for them.

The Artist garners speculation – what was he thinking to make us ponder his deepest thoughts mind to brush to palette to canvas? We gaze in awe at the twisted shapes of Picasso and the surrealism of Max Ernst not first seeing what their minds first saw, to the marvellously intuitive Caffe Greco of Renato Guttuso, and give our interpretation not knowing his.

The writer has a beginning, a middle and an end – their interpretation becomes ours, not so the artist. Both genres make us think and probe to discuss making our eyes light up with the glow of eventual understanding, and then we know.

Artists and Writers philosophers both – we came we saw we thought and then we did.

IPA writer's group following a visit to Cologne on a Wednesday in November 2019. The International Police Association (IPA) writer's group were tasked to record their impressions following a day visit to Cologne.

15

The Unmarked Grave

The young captain in the South African army had been in it from the beginning.

He and his two brothers had signed up on the day that war was declared in September 1939 and had been part of the East African campaign, driving the Germans and Italians ever Northwards until eventually they had retreated from the hot sands of North Africa. In Abysinnia (Ethiopia), the sole South African division had faced numerous divisions of Italian troops and had totally crushed the Italian army in that country. Now, some three years later, they were ready for the big push into Europe, landing at Anzio in Italy. Some of the fiercest fighting was around Monte Casino and the division took heavy casualties. The young captain was one of them. He had taken shrapnel from a shell burst across his back and his legs and found himself some five days later in a field hospital, somewhere behind the Allied lines.

The Unmarked Grave

After some time convalescing at a chateau, commandeered by the army in the south of Italy, he was still not fit enough for active service, despite being keen to get back into action. Although South African, he was also Jewish and his driving ambition was to see the war through against the hated Nazis. Thus it was, when the hospital ship set off for Cape Town, he stayed behind, having requested further orders to be involved. Eventually, these came through. His excitement when ripping open the envelope containing his force movement orders turned to one of total dismay when he read that he had been posted as a Unit Commander on attachment to the War Graves Commission with the job of locating soldiers and airman who had died in battle and lay in unmarked graves.

"This is not my idea of fighting a war", he thought. "Surely someone else can do this job." However, there was no way of changing the orders, and he set out to the War Graves Commission offices in Rome. There, they redirected him back to the Southern sector to take up his command.

Blondie Requited

This was a six - month post. For the first five months he followed up any leads on where soldiers had fallen in battle and been hastily buried. The job of his team was to exhume these bodies and identify them, mostly removing them to specially-designated military cemeteries for re-interment. He couldn't say that he enjoyed the job. In fact, he absolutely hated it. Unlike most soldiers who have long periods of idleness, followed by sudden spurts of activity, this to him was the ultimate drudge. Each day, he knew he would be facing the harsh reality of death. Sometimes bodies were booby trapped and sometimes he came across gross atrocities where wounded soldiers had been executed on the battlefield. All of his findings were meticulously recorded, as ingrained in his legal mind, with evidence collected and assimilated to be used, if required, against the enemy after the war had ended.

One day the unit received information from the Italian partisans in a remote area, about an allied aircraft which had crashed on a hilltop some months previously. They were told that the partisans, had buried the bodies on the hill. The captain and his driver quickly set out in the open

The Unmarked Grave

army jeep for Consiglio, which was about 120 miles to the North. It was a warm, pleasant day, and the rich aromatic smells rising from freshly turned turf as they drove through the farming areas and vineyards, produced a calming effect on them both. The fighting had long since moved further North and there was no longer danger now in this area. The occupying forces had produced a military administration and infrastructure to reorganise the country and enable ordinary people to begin living their lives again. It was no secret that most Italians did not support the Germans occupying their country, despite Italy being allies of the Germans.

A few hours later, the young captain and his driver arrived at the village of Consiglio, nestling at the foothills of a mountain range. His first job was to find the local mayor to ask for directions to get to the scene of the incident where the two airmen lay buried. Everyone seemed to know the general direction, but no-one was prepared to take them there, until a young boy offered to lead them to the base of a small hill just north of the town. The youngster leapt into the back of the jeep and the captain and his driver wound their way upwards along the dirt track, closely following the directions of the young boy. When they reached the base of the hill, the driver stopped the jeep and the Captain got out to survey what lay before him. The hill was about six hundred metres high and, through his binoculars, he could see it would be a long hot a climb, particularly as the sun had been slowly rising and was now at its zenith. The boy refused to go any further, saying that the Germans had planted anti-personnel mines all around its slopes, and no-one knew where they were. The young captain took his binoculars and began walking around the side of the hill looking for the best route to the top. He would stop every couple of metres and sweep the slopes with his binoculars, moving ever further away from the driver and the boy. He had almost rounded the side of the hill when a man walked up to him saying that he knew the way through the minefield and would take him to where the bodies were buried. The man was dressed in army fatigues and introduced himself as Lt. Fisher. It was not uncommon at that time to have military detachments, either resting up in rear areas or patrolling the country, looking for fugitives.

"Are you sure you know the way, as I believe the hill is mined?" asked the Captain.

"Yes, I've been up there many times as the views from the top of the hill over the valley are the best in the area," the man replied.

The captain adjusted his entrenching tool to the small haversack which he carried on his back and he set off after Fisher up the hill. Usually, his driver helped him in marking the graves, especially when there was digging to do, but in this case the driver was out of earshot and as he had company anyway, he didn't bother to call him. However, he knew that his driver would be watching their progress up the hill.

Although Fisher seemed to know the way and was diagonally traversing the hill, the young captain, being cautious, was however playing out a white roll of tape which he had carried in his haversack leaving a trail behind him. Thus, if anyone else needed to get up the hill through the minefield, at least they would have an easy marked path to follow.

The sun was now at its highest, burning down with the summer intensity, which added to the pain of his healing wounds, had slowed him down. He had to call out to Fisher to slow his pace, which the other man did briefly. Fisher was moving with an urgency now which was difficult to comprehend, as if he was actually desperate to get there. The captain knew that he had to conserve his energy, as he was not long out of hospital and needed a slower pace.

Half way up the hill, he stopped and turned, surveying the scene with his binoculars. Way down below, he could see the driver waving to him and he waved back. Having caught his breath, he turned around and followed on up the hill after Fisher.

The Unmarked Grave

The scenery was different now. The verdant farmlands far below had changed to a rocky, almost stark outlook, with the odd twisted olive tree interspersed with tufts of grass and heather. He saw no sign of life at all, no birds, no small animals, nothing. He had counted five anti-personnel mines on the way up which had been dislodged by recent heavy rains over the past couple of months and suspected that there must have been many more which he hadn't seen. He thought it was just as well that he had brought the marking tape which now zigzagged behind him as he painstakingly made his way upwards and onwards.

When he reached the top of the hill, Fisher was already there with his hands on his hips. He could sense the impatience of the man, anxious to get on.

"Do you know where the graves actually are?" the Captain asked Fisher.

"Of course I do, I told you I've been here before", he said, walking towards two mounds of earth with rocks placed on top them. Already grass was growing right across both the mounds and a solitary stick stood between them, which must have been left by the partisans when they buried the bodies which they had found. There was no visible sign anywhere of the wreckage of the aircraft. The captain thought this was really strange, as he bent down to examine the graves. "Do you know where the aircraft crashed"? he asked Fisher. Fisher explained that it had gone down on the other side of the hill and he thought the partisans had brought the bodies back to the top of the hill to bury them.

The Captain consulted his file. There was only a reported sighting of an aircraft that had gone down, "Place unknown" following a dog fight with a Messerschmidt 109. Many aircraft had gone missing in this way, when their radio communications had failed or been shot out and, as a result, the air force had no idea of the exact location. A squadron of planes may have taken off from an airfield many miles away, been involved in aerial combat and sustained half a dozen losses. It was only by painstakingly

The Unmarked Grave

putting together the pieces of the jigsaw on the ground, that some of these mysteries were ever solved.

He turned to Fisher and gave him the entrenching tool, as he had offered to dig the soil out of the grave. The Captain was pleased for the respite as the climb up the hill had severely weakened him. Eventually, the first grave was uncovered to reveal the skeletal remains of the pilot lying there. Fisher stood back as the young captain reached down for the dog tags which would identify the pilot to him. These were round metal discs, secured around the neck of the deceased with a metal chain, not unlike a plug stopper for a bath.

The Captain was now on his knees at the side of the grave, his perspiration mingling with the dust on his face and forearms and dripping down below him. He reached forward and grasped the silver chain in his hand and snapped it with one quick easy motion. He lifted the tags up to his eyes and wiped away the accumulated dirt so that he could see what secrets would be revealed to him about the identity of the fallen airman.

"Hey, that's a coincidence, this chap has exactly the same name as you", he said, slowly getting to his feet and turning around. There was no sign of Fisher. The young captain felt the hairs on the nape of his neck begin to rise and stand out stiffly as his body went cold. A tingling sensation ran across his forearms and down his spine. He called out Fisher's name, there was no response. There was no sign of him. He thought that it was odd that Fisher had not waited but maybe had probably gone on ahead, thinking that the job had been done. However, this was totally out of character as Fisher had been keen and enthusiastic to get to the site of the grave, only to disappear now once it was uncovered. It was most odd.

The young Captain re-interred the body, marking it with the special War Graves plaque to indicate that it had been found, recorded and tagged. He then walked back towards the edge of the hill from whence he came. He took out his binoculars and again examined the scene beneath him. There was no sign of any other human or animal presence on this side of the hill. He realised that had he not laid out the white marker tape through the minefield, he would never have been sure of getting back safely without being blown up. Although the experience had unnerved him, for some reason he felt extraordinarily light-headed and happy. After winding his way back down the hill, following the white tape he had earlier rolled out to mark the way through the minefield, he eventually reached the jeep and his driver.

The driver remarked 'you were very lucky not to get blown up by an AP mine on your way up the hill'. The Captain replied that it wasn't so much luck but that he had a guide named Lt. Fisher leading him up the hill. The driver retorted 'I was watching you all the way with the binoculars and there was no one with you at all'. 'Are you sure' asked the Captain, as another chill swept through his body. It suddenly dawned on the Captain that Lt. Fisher had actually led him to his own grave through a dangerous minefield.

16

War Poetry – Denis Rhodes Granger in the Western Desert

My father Denis Rhodes Granger was born in Southern Rhodesia on 11 November 1911. His father Joseph Granger was a contemporary of Cecil Rhodes, who became Prime Minister of the Cape in South Africa and Denis was named after him. The country itself was barely 20 years old when he was born. At the age of 7 he was sent to boarding school at Wynberg BHS in the Cape, South Africa with a train ticket tied around his neck. After school Denis qualified as a lawyer and practised law in Worcester, South Africa.

He signed up on 3 September 1939 the day war was declared with his two brothers Edgar and Vincent Granger. He was 27 at the time and practising law as an attorney in Worcester, South Africa. At the outset of WW2 Denis joined the 6th South African division on their campaigns through East Africa, Abyssinia and North Africa, before going on to Italy. He transferred over to the British Army in Egypt as an intelligence officer, and as a young lieutenant joined a certain Captain David Stirling working as part of the SOE (Special Operations Executive), later to form the SAS. Denis was parachuted behind enemy lines in Yugoslavia, Crete and other theatres of war on a number of missions. One was to bring out two German sea captains who had surrendered, another to support the partisans.

In the Western Desert, on another mission, he was captured by the Italians when he and his driver drove into a supposedly unoccupied wadi and found themselves surrounded by enemy tanks. That night they managed to escape. On another occasion he was captured by the Gestapo in Eastern Europe who broke his fingers under interrogation – on this occasion he was rescued by partisans who broke open the prison to free their own leader who was also being held captive. He was later mentioned in despatches for distinguished service published in the London Gazette on 23 May 1946 which reads 'Captain Granger has been informed that his award was for gallant and distinguished services for the period to June 1944'.

Denis remained in the army as a territorial after the War in both South Africa and Rhodesia and was subsequently called up in his sixties to command one of the 2 Brigade

Units during the Rhodesian Bush war. Whilst we were often on duty at the same time, we only ever met up once in the bush, on the Zambezi escarpment. This was near a petrified forest and we both collected a piece of tree solidified into rock – eventually these ended up on the mantelpiece in each of our homes.

Dad was an excellent rifle shot represented South Africa for Western Province and Rhodesia at Bisley. His brother Vincent, in his memoirs wrote *'My brother Denis, too, was an outstanding rifleman. Indeed, as a young man he won the floating trophy for the highest individual score at Western Cape Command's Bisley in Bellville. The historic shield with all its silver badges proudly graced our mantelpiece for a year when we lived in Kenilworth'*. He qualified with a sniper marksman badge during WW2.

Denis played most sports at school, but shone at cricket, rugby and shooting. Denis played provincial cricket for Griqualand West and North-Western Districts in South Africa and rugby for Griquas. A cutting from a newspaper in the mid 1930s shows a somewhat stubborn approach to cricket. Griquas in the first innings scored 372 for 7 wickets declared. Whilst playing for North-Western Districts they were all out for 22 in their first innings, and 190 in the second innings, of which Denis scored 51. Official comment: *'Granger was at the crease for just over 7 hours and scored only four 4's... Granger used his pads and a dead bat with advantage against the spinners in particular and survived constant l.b.w. appeals.... I spoke to Denis Granger after the match and he told me that he had been coached as an opening bat at Wynberg BHS in Cape Town by Jack Newman, the Hampshire professional who was an exponent of the use of pads in defence...'*

Generally apolitical, he had a strong sense of right and wrong. He was arrested and locked up allegedly for spying by President Mugabe's CIO, when he had gone to photograph the scene of a bus accident at Seki for an insurance claim, as he was the attorney for the insurance company. He later sued the Zimbabwe Government for wrongful arrest and won his case and was awarded damages – of course never paid! I asked him if he ever received the damages owing and he said he deducted what was owed to him from his tax bill until it was paid off. He had challenged the Zimbabwe Government's Emergency Powers in the Supreme Court alleging 'unlawful and injurious conduct' by members of the CIO, which he won. No one in the family knew he had been arrested, and my mother thought he was on a trip at the time as he was often away on Lions Club (he was a Charter Member of Lions in Rhodesia) or masonic functions. His wife, my mother Isabeau, was attending a dinner at the University of Rhodesia when one of Denis's colleagues mentioned how sorry he was to hear that he had been arrested, which came as quite a shock.

After WW2 he was one of South Africa's legal representatives at the Nuremberg Trials for war criminals, and only returned to South Africa in 1947. Having fought for the freedom of people around the world, he became involved in various anti- apartheid legal actions, including representing the Coloured people when they were disenfranchised by the new Nationalist Government. Even though constitutional cases were won by the claimants, the Government kept introducing new legislation to enforce separate development of the various racial groups. Increasingly disillusioned, he returned to Rhodesia to practise law in the late 1950s.

War Poetry – Denis Rhodes Granger in the Western Desert

Highly accomplished, Denis was at one time the President of the Federation of Amateur Theatrical Societies of South Africa, his plays making it to the finals at national festival level. He also adjudicated school plays – and at the age of 87 he acted in a panto produced by his daughter Angela for the Marlborough Players. Denis presented acting cups to my school – Sinoia High School - and maintained a great interest in theatre. He was also theatre critic for the Citizen and Sunday Mail. He met my mother Isabeau, who acted in many of his plays, through the theatre. He even appeared in film, playing the part of Scarface in the black and white movie production of David Copperfield, filmed during WW2.

Denis turned his literary endeavours to poetry on more than one occasion. He wrote an anthology of 'Service Verse' much along the lines of Swinburne and Kipling, much of it based in East Africa, The Middle East and Italy, where he had seen war service. His poetry takes us from Sonderwater training camp near Pretoria in June 1940, up to Nairobi in Kenya, Gulu and Moyale in Uganda, during 1940 and then in 1941 back to Kenya. He then moved to Kufra Oasis in 1942 where he joined Popski in action destroying German planes on the ground; being caught in a

Khamseen sand storm in the Western Desert in 1942, up to Egypt in May 1944 (the poem was published in the Army Newspaper 'Union Jack' about an American Army jeep being awarded the purple heart after being battle scarred in numerous campaigns).

Poems then follow in Italy during 1943 and 1944, as well as London in 1944, the anthology finally ending in the Zambezi Valley in September 1969. I have selected one of his poems below:

Khamseen

The convoy rested in the early dawn

The sun peered cool over the sterile sand,

Boots stirred the pale enamelled shells of snails

The whited sepulchres of aeons long past,

And crushed, the brittle aromatic sage

Perfumed the air.

The little creatures of the desert came

War Poetry – Denis Rhodes Granger in the Western Desert

To suck the early dew from withered thorn;

Travel worn the soldiers sipped hot tea

Then slept. The reaching fingers of the sun

Warmed the shy lizards and the beetles brown,

That drowsy morn.

But then the distance fades to misty grey

A dark cloud pulls across the waning sun

The dawn breeze whimpers and then fades away.

We moved the trucks together and secure

Tight canvas tops. The outposts are recalled

And then we wait.

There is an hush before the angry wind

With whirling eddies pitilessly hurl

Stones with harsh drum-beats on protesting iron.

The timid creatures of the desert flee

Blondie Requited

Before the anger of the raging storm

We call Khamseen'

Western Desert 1942

Glossary

BSAP	-	British South Africa Police (Rhodesian police force)
Gweru	-	was Gwelo
Harare	-	was Salisbury
Inyanga	-	now Nyanga
Inyangani	-	now Nyangani
IPA	-	International Police Association
Oom	-	Uncle (Afrikaans)
Rhodesia	-	now Zimbabwe
Rooiaas	-	red bait (Afrikaans)
SA	-	South Africa
Salisbury	-	now Harare
SB	-	Special Branch
Sinoia	-	now Chinoyi
Umtali	-	now Mutare
WW2	-	World War 2 (1939 – 1945)
Zimbabwe	-	was Southern Rhodesia then Rhodesia

Epilogue

I am indebted to the many characters who have made this book of short stories possible, many of them totally unaware that they feature in central or cameo parts in it until they read the book, bringing pleasure to the host of readers who have had the courage to fork out good money for this. No offence is intentionally caused to anyone alive or dead, and in certain instances I have changed the names although the stories are true, or as related to me where they may not be.

I like to have a thread of humour or amazement throughout the book. Wow did that really happen? Part of the magic of writing is to tell a good story, and of course the author has a certain amount of poetic licence when doing so. I am indebted to my sister Debbie Alvord for often saying ' it didn't really happen like that' and to my sons who agree with her that I can exaggerate a tiny bit. They are quite right of course – one has to 'up the ante' when story telling. In all other areas I have researched the facts and modern technology has played its part in assisting me. For example, I was neatly side-tracked when trying to determine the exact weight of a mealie bag to be carried by a Free State farmer when training for rugby. I happened upon a thread describing the size of mealie bags used in the barricade at Rorke's drift (posted by Peter Ewart in 2012 in RDVC Forums), part of which shows:

Degacher's coloured sketch of part of the barricade, which de Neuville used when planning his painting, shows four biscuit boxes and well over a dozen sacks jammed into the spaces beneath, around and on top of one of the wagons. Any questions about the actual size of the sacks when filled can be answered by this illustration, drawn from life within hours of the action and additionally helpful by our being able to compare them with the known size of the wagon. With regard to any markings on either sacks or boxes, *Degacher included none*. Looking at this well known sketch, it could be argued that he paid more attention to their outline than to texture or markings, but it seems certain that de Neuville discussed their appearance with him before painting his own bags and boxes.

Because de Neuville's composition views the action from within the perimeter, we see only a handful of filled sacks scattered in disarray. But they *are* in the immediate foreground and they are painted in sufficient detail to clearly indicate their size (and perhaps even weight). They are close enough for us to examine carefully the stitching, the colour, stains, smudges and even stitched repairs. *There are no markings at all on de Neuville's mealie sacks*. Four or five large, wooden boxes, identically shaped and sized, also litter his foreground, the nearest of which bears the words "Commissariat – Navy Biscuit" stamped or stencilled on its side. To me, this smacks not of artist's licence but of authenticity, given that these are not necessarily the words the public might initially have expected to see. De Neuville had already spoken to those who knew. But what also seem to be the words "Rorke's Drift .. Natal" might appear to question this supposition – this time suggesting licence – especially as between these words the semblance of a possible date can just be seen, indicating 22 or 22nd!

If so, perhaps the artist included this "symbol" as some sort of historical signature to his composition?

In the second of these 1880 "heavyweights", Lady B depicts boxes in only the far distant background, alongside the mealie redoubt, so no conclusion can be drawn from her work on this point. However, very prominent in the close foreground are four or five large mealie sacks, and these appear to be completely plain apart from the one protecting John Williams/Fielding. It seems to be stamped with the letters "S O" or perhaps "S C" – or, if we're meant to look at it upside down (why not?) perhaps even "P S." Any guesses on the meaning of these letters? Just as interesting in her painting of the sacks is another distinctive marking on all four bags running along the top of her foreground perimeter. She depicts three thin, parallel lines, a central blue (possibly black?) one between two red ones running along the whole length of each sack. This may, or may not, be intended to represent stitching – at least the central, darker line might – but I doubt it. The lines are quite carefully and deliberately included on each nearby sack, including the one underneath a wounded soldier, far right. Has this eminent artist, in a painting well known for her attention to detail, suddenly made these lines up? Or has she spoken to someone who described them? Or if she, too, has decided to include a symbolic marker for her patron, The Queen, did she choose these red and blue lines for that purpose? By coincidence, Gibb's "The Thin Red Line" was being painted at that very time!

From this description I was no further enlightened, however had an excellent description of a mealie bag or sack as seen by various artists.

I have included amongst the stories a different type of writing following my visit to Cologne with the IPA writers' group comparing a writer to a painter, which I enjoyed doing – it made me think about something different from an artistic point of view. Whichever the reader's preference I am hopeful that this collection of short stories will be enjoyed by many.

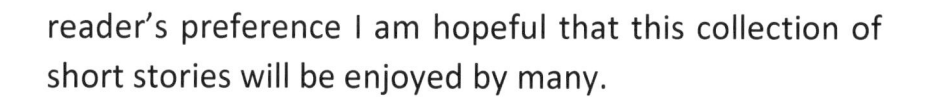

Tony Granger

Shrewsbury

November 2020

If you have enjoyed reading Blondie Requited then please order Blondies Revenge at www.tonygrangerauthor.com or by emailing tonygranger@hotmail.com